WHIP ME

A collection of twenty erotic stories

Edited by Cathryn Cooper

Published by Accent Press Ltd – 2007
ISBN 1905170920 / 9781905170920

Printed and bound in the UK by
Creative Design and Print

Cover Design by
Red Dot Design

Also available from Xcite Books:
(www.xcitebooks.com)

Sex & Seduction	**1905170785**	**price £7.99**
Sex & Satisfaction	**1905170777**	**price £7.99**
Sex & Submission	**1905170793**	**price £7.99**
5 Minute Fantasies 1	**1905170610**	**price £7.99**
5 Minute Fantasies 2	**190517070X**	**price £7.99**
5 Minute Fantasies 3	**1905170718**	**price £7.99**
Whip Me	**1905170920**	**price £7.99**
Spank Me	**1905170939**	**price £7.99**
Tie Me Up	**1905170947**	**price £7.99**
Ultimate Sins	**1905170599**	**price £7.99**
Ultimate Sex	**1905170955**	**price £7.99**
Ultimate Submission	**1905170963**	**price £7.99**

Contents

Discipline
by Sommer Marsden

I remember saying it to him. I remember it clearly. My first book was out, my second in the works. I had a looming deadline and absolutely no fire under my ass to make any sort of progress.

I would panic, calm down, and bitch. But I could not throw myself into my work. I was on the verge of tossing my laptop into the bathtub and turning on the faucet when Austin walked in.

'Babe? What's wrong? You've got the crazy hair from running your fingers through it.'

Normally Austin's warm, deep voice and easy smile were enough to take me off edge. It didn't work.

'I need discipline!' I blurted out. 'I am the most undisciplined person I know. I have exactly ten and a half days to wrap up this manuscript and turn it in.' I gave my hair one more raking for good measure and let my head thunk on the desk. I would wallow in self pity. It wouldn't help, but I would do it anyway.

Austin rubbed my back and neck and gave a little chuckle. 'Then finish it, Lizzie. Just finish it.'

That put my hackles up. 'I can't! It's right there. I mean, it is right there in my head, all ready but...'

'But?'

'No fire. No fire to write. I'm content to let it sit there all ready and waiting until the deadline is screaming in my ear. Then the fire will be there and as usual, I will be flying by the seat of my pants. It sucks.'

'Change it.'

'I can't.'

'Ah, you won't, is what you mean.'

I hated when he called me on something. It was even worse when the something was a character flaw that I truly loathed.

'Fine,' I grumped, 'I won't.'

'We'll have to do something about that,' he said on his way out of my office.

'What?'

He just smiled.

Six days left until my deadline. I clicked my email icon. I checked my website. I checked my favourite blogs. All the while, I mentally calculated. I had thirty thousand words left to meet my length requirement. I had six days. That was an average of five thousand words or more each day. Panic swelled in my chest, making my head swim and my ears ring. Yet, I didn't open the document containing my novel. Instead I went to my favourite used-books website and looked around.

Austin popped his head in. 'Super busy or you up for some grocery shopping?' His dark brown eyes found the website and he grinned and shook his head. 'I guess super busy is out.'

I sighed. 'Sure. Let's go. Maybe realising that we'll no longer be able to buy food if I don't finish this fucking book will give me the kick in the ass I need.'

'I don't think you need a kick in the ass,' he said, reaching for my hand. 'You need something, but not to be kicked.'

'What do I need?'

'I have an idea, but it's a secret. Let's go. Errands! It'll be fun.'

'Fun,' I muttered and let him hug me. I put my hand in the back pocket of his faded jeans and gave his ass a squeeze. 'Maybe a good romp in the sack will get me fired up.'

'We might have to give it a try,' he said, walking me to the front door. He handed me my jacket and then pulled me in for a hug. 'You trust me, right?'

'Of course.' Had I been that down? That snippy? For him to think that I no longer trusted him? 'I love you and I trust you. You know that, right?'

'Yep,' he said, winking. 'Just needed to hear you say it. Now let's get our errands done and see if we can help Lizzie with her self-imposed writer's block.'

'I'm not blocked, just lazy,' I sighed, climbing into the car.

'Not lazy,' he corrected, 'you were right. You just need a little discipline.'

For some reason when he said it, a little tingle swept up my spine followed by a satisfying shiver. And a tiny touch of arousal. Confusing but true. I let it go. Time to focus on groceries and then on my issues with working like a normal person.

I shuffled through our errands and tried to mentally digest knocking out five thousand words. And then doing it again. And again. I was getting more distressed with each stop we made. Finally, after dropping off overdue books at the library, Austin turned to me and patted my leg.

'Ready to go home and have a fire lit under your ass?'

Zing! There was that arousal again. What was wrong with me? On top of being a top-notch procrastinator, I was getting turned on by his completely innocent comments. I

3

gulped and shook my head a little to clear it. 'Sure. You have a plan?'

'Yes, Lizzie, I do,' he said and then quickly tweaked my nipple through my thin hoodie. 'I have several plans.' The normally warm look in Austin's eyes now bordered on dangerous. His gaze darker and more intense than I had ever seen it.

'OK,' I managed, though to my own ears my voice was unstable at best.

'Let's go.'

I pondered his comment all the way home. What did he mean? Surely, he wouldn't... hurt me. Never. Austin would never hurt me. Ever. I knew that for a fact. However, denying the look I had seen on his face was stupid. I had seen it. After seven years, I knew his facial expressions. I could honestly say that I had never seen that particular look before. And it excited me. A lot. The nipple he had pinched was still hard and sensitive. The other one was simply hard for moral support.

'You go up and get undressed. I'll be there once I unload the car,' Austin said it as if he were asking me to shut the car door for him.

'What? I'll help. We can both unload the car and–'

Austin turned to me slowly and let his eyes roam my body for a second. Then he levelled his gaze and stared me right in the eyes. 'I said, go up and get undressed. Wait for me. Take everything off. I will be up as soon as I've unloaded the car.'

He said it quietly and slowly and each new word he threw out into the air sent another jolt of excitement from deep in my belly to the now wet place between my thighs.

'O-Okay.'

'Good girl. Go on. Hurry up.' And then he turned his back to me.

4

I felt dazed. Confused. I made my way upstairs and tried not to turn it over too much in my head. I trusted him. I had always trusted him. I would trust him now. Plus, I would be a liar if I said that my whole body was not radiating a pleasant, tingling anticipation. My cunt was already wet. Nipples hard. The smooth skin of my belly fluttered just from the friction of my denim waistband as I moved. I shivered when I pulled the ocean blue hoodie over my head and dropped it to the floor. Next my pink bra. Jeans. Lacy white thong. Socks. Shoes.

Then I sat on the edge of the bed and waited. I held my knees together, my spine straight, ankles crossed. Austin hadn't told me how to sit and I felt uncertain. Realising what a completely bizarre thought that was, I giggled. Austin would never tell me how I was supposed to sit. Or how to do anything else for that matter.

But he just ordered you upstairs and stripped naked and waiting... and you listened.

Another shiver, another pulse of excitement, another streak of liquid between my thighs. All true. I waited. I was cold. I sat. I didn't know what to do, so I sat patiently and waited.

He made me wait forever. Austin is quick but surefooted. He moves fast, talks fast, works fast and thinks fast. The only time he is languid and slow is in the bedroom. There he sees fit to take his time. Relish our acts and our time together. I adore that side of him. This time, as I waited I could hear him moving methodically downstairs. He seemed to be deliberately pacing himself. To make me wait. To draw out the excitement. It worked.

By the time he finally appeared in the doorway, it was a struggle to keep my spine straight. My knees kept banging together no matter how hard I tried to keep them still. My heart beat so rapidly I felt almost sick and my ears felt stuffed full of cotton. Worst of all, I was positive that I had created a nice sized wet stain beneath me. My pussy was so slick and impatient it just kept generating more and more lubricant for the cock it so desperately awaited.

'I like that,' Austin said almost nonchalantly. He nodded at my posture and gave me a very small, smile. 'Nice. You look like you'll catch on quickly to this discipline thing.' As he spoke he pulled down the blinds on all three windows. Then he pulled the armchair from the corner of the bedroom and nodded. 'I want you here.'

I rose slowly, fighting a sudden and overwhelming light-headedness. I walked to the chair and sat, hoping not to stain the butter-coloured brocade with my fluids. Austin shook his head and twirled his finger in the air.

'The other way. Knees on the cushions. Arms on the back of the chair. Forehead on your arms. Legs spread wide so your knees touch the inside of the arms. Your weight will be spread evenly. You won't lose your balance.'

'Lose my balance? Austin what—'

'Time to listen and not speak, Lizzie. I will not tell you again.'

There it was again, I realised as I changed position. That surge of fear tinged with pleasure. I was out of my comfort zone but in hands that I trusted. The fear and the arousal were a heady mix. I swayed a little as I turned. Austin's big, warm hands pushed the insides of my knees until the outsides of my thighs bumped the padded arms of the chair. He pulled my forearms back a little so they were evenly on the headrest and crossed them. Then he pushed my head down a little further. This forced my ass out. Out in the air. Vulnerable. Then his finger pushed into me and I gasped out loud.

'I see that you have had plenty of time to anticipate. And think. And work yourself up.'

His laughter was soft and dark. Nearly sinister. And yet, I trusted. He would never hurt me. Not really.

6

'Choose a word,' he said. I could hear him removing his socks and his shirt. The soft whisper of fabric being folded and discarded.

'What?'

'A word. I would like you to choose a word. To keep you safe. A word that you will say if you truly want me to stop. At any time. What's the word?'

I didn't even thing. It popped right out of my mouth. 'Procrastinator.'

'Good choice, Lizzie. Because that word, related to you, is about to become a thing of the past.'

My skin rippled with goose bumps and I bucked involuntarily as if he had touched me again between my legs.

'Do you hear me, Lizzie?'

'Yes. I hear you.'

'Good girl.'

I heard the clank of his belt buckle, then the long sinuous sound of the wide leather being withdrawn from the denim loops. 'See, when I was a little boy, before my dad left us, I got whippings.'

My nipples seized up and I couldn't seem to swallow or speak. I was ready to blurt out the word right then and there but all that came from between my lips was an airless, hollow sound.

'When I did not do the things expected of me. Things I was *paid* good allowance money to do, he didn't take my allowance. He took the pay out of my hide. That's what he called it. Taking payment.'

I was paid to write. Paid fairly well, too.

He spoke directly in my ear on my left side. He hadn't touched me yet. I didn't raise my head or my eyes. From my position all I could see of him was his bare flat stomach, the belt in his hands, his denim clad legs and his bare feet. My heart jittered in my chest and I struggled for air.

7

'And I hated it. I hated him for doing it. It was humiliating and shameful and it pissed me off. I got better with my chores. I did things the way I was supposed to. I became faster and more efficient and more responsible. There was one thing I always noticed, though. I never admitted it to anyone. In fact, I've never spoken it out loud. Would you like to know what it is, Lizzie?' His fingers stroked my hair so softly that I couldn't believe he was talking about whipping me with his leather belt. The thought seemed ridiculous. But that was exactly what he was doing.

'Yes,' I said so softly I doubted he heard me.

'I noticed that when all was said and done. When he had left the room after collecting his payment, that I was hard. Every single time. Hard as a rock. And the moment I could get into the bathroom and lock that door, I jacked off. They were the best orgasms. Those pleasurable releases stained with pain.'

I felt a little sob well up in my throat. Now it wasn't because he was talking about whipping me. About intentionally striking me. It was because I realised I *wanted* him to. Very much.

I nodded but didn't speak.

'Are you willing to let me teach you some discipline? Make you a better writer? More efficient and conscientious?'

Another nod. Another shiver. Another trickle of fluid down my inner thighs.

'Good. Remember your word and count them off for me. I won't hurt you too much, Lizzie. He did it to hurt me. I'm doing it to help and to give you something you've never had before. That release. You trust me?'

This time I spoke aloud. 'With my life.'

'For this first time, we'll start with ten.'

8

He touched my hair one more time. Very softly. Reverently. Then he positioned himself behind me and I felt myself tense. I had never tensed up around Austin. I had never felt the need. With this new experience looming over me, I tensed. Thrust into a new sexual arena I felt a clawing terror in my chest mixed with curiosity and desire. I wanted this. To feel what it was like. To put myself in his hands.

What you see in the movies is real. That whistle through the air. The shift of oxygen molecules. I felt the stinging bite of leather on my skin before my ears picked up the sound. The overwhelmingly loud *crack!* of it biting into my skin. The sound of my pain tore out of my throat as my body bucked in the chair. Breasts banging the back of the chair, legs twitching involuntarily.

'One,' I sobbed and then wondered how I would weather nine more.

The second one connected in a different place with a different sound. Higher on my buttocks, overlapping to some degree flesh that had already been traumatized.

'Two.' I gritted my teeth when I said it but there was a hint of scream in my voice. I wanted to scream. I wanted to cry. I wanted to beg. And I wanted him to go on.

By the time we hit five, my face was doused with salty tears. They ran off my forearms in little rivers. My ass was on fire. Throbbing agony that made way into softer flickers of pain. This wasn't to hurt me, I reminded myself. Austin's father had meant to hurt him. What must *that* have felt like?

The next blow was so much lighter than the others. A kiss of the leather across my pulsing bottom. 'Six,' I said. It was almost a sigh. So pleasurable now. It had... had... what? Felt good. The pulse of my abused skin had reached my cunt and I felt it constricting with anticipation.

Each one got a little lighter then as my counting grew to moans of pleasure. 'Seven...eight...nine...' I had relaxed

9

into the chair. My weight rested on my head and my ass was raised almost whorishly.

I heard the belt whistle but I was too late. That had been a tease. The final one was for real but my body wasn't ready. It ripped across my flesh with a vengeance, igniting every nerve in my body. Burning them up with fierce, toothy pain.

'Ten!' I shrieked and collapsed, sobbing against the chair.

The belt thudded to the floor and his hands were on me. He smoothed them over my bottom, so softly it felt like an air current. His mouth found my ear and dropped a wet kiss there. Then on to behind my ears. My neck.

' I am so very proud of you,' he whispered. Even though I was still wracked with sobs, I couldn't help the smile or the swell of pride.

His fingers pushed into me. One finger, two fingers, three. I gasped and pushed back against him. Felt my body clench hungrily around his digits. Felt the beautiful light of pleasure swirl up my insides and settle somewhere around my ribcage.

'Lizzie?'

'Hmmm?' I pushed back against his hand, forcing his fingers deeper. He knew my body so well. He hooked his fingers and stroked my G-spot.

'Do you feel the difference?' As he spoke, he probed with his fingers and smoothed his other hand over the still-throbbing flesh of my bottom.

'Yes. Yes, I do.'

'Good.' Now he was gentle, pushing the blunt head of his swollen cock between my slick folds, finding my entrance. He slid into me slowly. Just the head first. Then a little more. My body stretched then pulled. Pulsing around him. Beckoning him deeper. Right at the end he thrust hard and high. All the way into me. I cried out as the first orgasm shot through me. Just like that. One hard thrust and it rocketed up through me until I felt as if my ears were burning and my head was swimming. He pushed in gently and pulled out slowly and let me ride the long, slippery waves of pleasure that didn't seem as if they would end.

Very gently he smacked my bruised skin and thrust hard again. Smaller, but just as intense, a second orgasm pulsed through my body. I hadn't even recovered from the first.

'So beautiful,' he said, finding a rhythm now as I pushed back to meet him. I wanted to soak him up. Take him all the way into me. The beautiful feel of his body in mine was like a drug. 'You were gorgeous. Counting them off, taking the blows. Your back bowed and shaking. Your ass striped and welted and angry red. But you did it,' he growled, his motions growing faster. 'So much more brave than I ever was. A fucking warrior. One who should never be afraid of her own talent. Never try to hide from it,' he grunted.

As soon as he said it I came. The truth. It was the truth. I felt overwhelmed at times, so I ran away. Hid from what I wanted to do with my life and my words. Austin came with me, yanking my hips so hard I screamed as my bruised ass banged his hipbones.

Little dots of white light danced in my vision. I put my head down and took a deep breath, not wanting to break contact. Austin's body was still linked with mine, his diminished but still firm cock in my cunt. I wanted to stay here for just a minute more.

Finally, he placed kisses along my spine and across my upper back. Then he pulled free and started to dress. I turned and sat in the chair then promptly jumped up with a screech.

'Five thousand words, Lizzie. Right now. I'll make dinner,' he said, handing me my clothes.

I put them on slowly and watched his face. He smiled his normal smile at me. I felt something loosen in my chest.

'I'm going to do it right now,' I assured him.

He handed me a throw pillow from the bed. 'You'll need this.'

I couldn't help it, I laughed. 'Think I'll ever need a refresher course?' I asked, secretly hoping I would.

'We all need refresher courses from time to time. I'm sure you'll be needing one in the future.'

I didn't say it but I thought it. *Good.*

The Catnip Club
by Cathryn Cooper

Jungle rhythms screamed and pounded from beneath Shirley Anne's feet. The blues band down in the Catnip Club were belting out their first number. The vibrations shuddered across the floor, crept up her calves and made her thighs and her buttocks tremble. Even the delicate fabric of her underwear shivered against her flesh. She was aware that her breasts were quivering like two jellies just turned out from their moulds, but she was none too concerned about that.

The man who owned the club was circling her, the circles diminishing in size so that he got closer, his scent getting stronger.

She liked his scent; liked him too: couldn't help holding her shoulders back so that her nipples pressed against the thin fabric of her dress, couldn't help arching her spine so that the seams of her dress strained against the opulent voluptuousness of her buttocks.

Half hidden behind dark lashes, her eyes followed his progress. There was a certain arrogance to the way he held himself. His chin was high. His eyes regarded her from either side of an aquiline nose that ended in flaring nostrils.

He moved gracefully, and yet she detected something else beneath the suave, sophisticated surface. Something more vigorous. Something deeply decadent.

He was a handsome man, this Rene Brabonne who owned the Catnip Club in the heart of the old quarter of New Orleans. He was dark and sleek in his well-made clothes. He had the air of someone sure of his position, sure of his roots.

Because he wore no jacket, she could discern the shape of his arms beneath his cotton shirt. His bright mustard vest wrestled with the muscles of his chest. Its silk back gleamed with the effort of containing the understated muscularity of his body. He was lithe rather than broad.

She trembled with anticipation as he came to a standstill in front of her and a mix of maleness, cologne and silk seemed to envelope her.

At first, her heart quaked at his closeness. A kind of fear made her direct her gaze at the floor which still trembled with the music from the club below. It was as if she was not permitted to look at him. He could only look at her.

A sudden well of defiance rose within her. Holding herself that much more erect, she tilted her chin and boldly, her dark green eyes looked into his.

Almost as though he understood, his eyes twinkled. Like stars, she thought, stars fashioned from steel.

'What is your name, cherie?' His voice was deep, warm as brandy and tinged with the lilt of Louisiana Cajun that sounded as if it was struggling to be Paris French.

She swallowed the dryness in her throat.

'Shirley Anne Porter, sir.'

'So what brought you to New Orleans?'

She met his gaze. 'I need a different life. I thought I could get that here.'

He blew a puff of cigar smoke, slipping the cigar between his teeth, chewing it as he moved away from her

14

and sat himself down in a big leather chair behind an equally large cedar desk. He took the cigar from his mouth.

'Your looks could be your fortune, Shirley Anne, but what else can you do. Can you sing?'

A flock of butterflies seemed to take flight in Shirley Anne's stomach. 'Yes. I used to sing in Church. In the choir. Sometimes solo.'

Rene chuckled. 'We do not indulge in too much church music here, cherie, though some feel their sins are so great they need to attend confession occasionally. Sing. Sing for me.'

She paused seeking a suitable song. Eventually her voice rang out, full of emotion, full of soul and strangely suiting the tempo of the band playing in the club downstairs.

As the song came to an end, he got to his feet and came to her. He patted the concave area beneath her ribs. His free hand caressed her cheek.

'Creole. Mulatto,' he said, 'A mix of classical European and a hint of darkest, wildest Africa.'

She looked into his eyes and felt the colour rising in her cheeks. In his eyes she could see herself naked, her body stretched out, arms high above her head, chained to a wall, a whip reddening her flesh. She could almost feel his teeth upon her breasts and the thrust of his pelvis grinding against hers.

He looked at her knowingly. 'You see something in my eyes?'

She looked away and shook her head. 'I don't know.'

'Have you heard of voodoo?'

She nodded, a sudden cold shiver running down her spine.

'Do not worry. You will be safe here. No harm will befall you. Are you afraid?'

She managed to shake her head.

'Did anyone else offer you a job before you came here?'

15

'Yes.'

'Tell me.'

'I don't know his name. He had gold teeth and wore a white suit. He asked if I was willing to appear naked suspended in a cage over the bar of his club. I didn't like it. The girls there wore nothing except rubber corsets and black stockings. Their breasts were strapped up so that the nipples pointed forward. Their nipples were painted gold. I didn't want to do that.'

He leaned close. She felt his breath on her cheek. 'But I might like that. What would you do if I asked you to paint your nipples and display yourself half-naked in public?'

She couldn't speak. Her tongue cleaved to the roof of her mouth. She'd got through the small sum of money she'd brought with her and could no longer afford to be choosy about what she did for a living – within reason.

'As long as they only watch but don't touch,' she blurted.

It was out in an instant, without thought, without preamble.

'A good answer.' He nodded as he blew more cigar smoke into the air. 'So do it. But not right away. You need to practise. Here. I will pay you.' He gave her a bundle of bills. 'Do you have somewhere to stay?'

She shook her head. 'No. But I can find somewhere now I have this.'

'Stay here tonight. There's a room through there.' He indicated a large pane of glass. 'This is a two way mirror. Before you sleep, I want to see you perform for me. Will you do that?'

That smell of masculine sexuality. Of course she would do it. And of course the room was hers for the night.

She sighed. This was better than she'd expected.

The room took her breath away. In the centre was a bed with a golden brocade cover. White linen drapes hung from

16

a brass and blue coronet above its head. Cream closets decorated with ormolu fronds and sweeps, all gilded with pale green and gold, stood against a wall. Tall gas lamps on heavy tripods hissed in each corner. There was a low chest of drawers and chairs of gold brocade, their legs braced on ball and claw feet.

This was so opulent, worlds apart from what she was used to. If this was what was possible, she wanted more. Rene had left her wanting much more than a room. She'd wanted him. She now wanted satisfaction, but on her own terms.

She stripped off her clothes and caught sight of her reflection in a mirror. Her nipples were dark as ripe plums and hard as cherries. A thick bush of hair nestled between her legs. Her skin glistened and her eyes were bright with excitement. Her own image surprised her and strangely filled her with longing. She deserved to be desired.

The sound of applause resounded from the club below. She jerked her attention away from herself and the mirror. Rene had set her a task. If she wanted all this – and more – then she must be creative, original and entertaining. She searched the room for ideas, for props and for encouragement.

To the left of the window was a five foot high statue of a black footman holding a tray. He was beautifully made, his muscular body picked out in artistic relief. She ran her fingers down over his hard chest. A thought occurred to her.

She glanced at the two-way mirror and smiled, pursed her lips and blew him a kiss. Purposely bending over, legs slightly parted, her buttocks, and that dark, hairy patch between, exposed to his view, she removed the tray.

Just as she'd expected, the statue had the most beautifully formed hands. Her breathing quicker now, she got astride the spread hand. Two fingers stood up proud of the rest. Shirley eased herself down onto them, murmuring with delight as, unyielding they pushed their way into her.

Carefully at first, she began to ride him, her eyes half closed and a low moan escaping her throat.

His palm, like his fingers, was hard against her sex. The high plateaus and low indentations of his hand pressed relentlessly against her fleshy lips. This was selfish love for her lover made no demands for satisfaction, for kisses, for the slightest favour in return for his services.

Sighing with delight, she wriggled a little on his hard hand so that, soon, she could almost forget he had no life. No warmth. He was only very hard and always available.

As her arousal deepened, she closed her eyes and remembered Seth. She had left their bed in the early hours of the morning before he'd awakened. She knew she would miss him but hoped to find someone just as fulfilling, just as willing to give her what she wanted.

His dark body had been almost as hard as this stiff mannequin, but warmer, and the words he'd poured into her ear had added to her desire. She'd wanted his hands to cover her, she'd wanted to submit because in submitting he was hers and she was his. She'd let him tie her up, blindfold her and have her helpless whilst he'd taken his pleasure.

He'd tied her legs apart, thick ropes around her ankles securing her to the foot of the bed. Her legs open. Her wrists secured above her, her eyes blindfolded, yet even that had not been enough for him. He'd gagged her and placed headphones over her ears. Only her senses of smell and touch had remained. She had smelled his body, but only through touch had they truly communicated.

Like now, she thought, though there was sound and the only touch was that of a cold, hard hand, but if she closed her eyes…

She threw back her head as she rubbed at her nipples. This was something the statue could not do. He could and he would bring her to orgasm, just by her manipulating her sex over his hand. In her mind it was him – or perhaps Seth – or perhaps even Rene playing with her nipples. She could pretend and, in pretending, the nub of tingling circling her clitoris began to spread like a web throughout her body.

A starburst of orgasm exploded from that tiny, sensitive spot nestling in her velvety folds. It was over! It was done. The statue had done its work. The pleasure, the release was all hers, except…

She opened her eyes and looked at the mirror. She smiled. Rene was on the other side. She knew the job, the accommodation and all that went with it was hers for the taking. And night after night, he would watch her hoping for a repeat performance, and there would be many. Her new lover was untiring in his ministrations. He would always be giving and in return she would give him nothing.

20

Yellow Decadence
by D J Kirkby

The afterglow from their time together yesterday afternoon still shone from her entire being, especially noticeable in her sparkling eyes and ready smile. There was nothing more exhilarating than rampant lovemaking with the man she absolutely adored; of that fact, if of little else in her life, she was certain. They had both been so busy recently that not finding time to make love had, sadly, begun to become a habit.

Yesterday he had gotten up early, preoccupied with trying to finish painting under the stairs, and Susan, never one to be outdone, had set herself the task of turning over the flower beds. The sun was warm on her face and back as she dug into the damp soil; wet clods of it falling off the spade, wafting a clay scent upwards. While raking the last of the winter debris from the lawn, she realised that she found the rocking motion of her legs and hips stimulating, a none-too-subtle reminder of their dry spell.

Distracted, she stopped and, leaning on the rake, stared at the bright yellow forsythia blossom to the side of the shed. It could do with a bit of a prune and she had a fabulous idea about what to do with the cuttings!

She set to work with a smile on her face, a throbbing clitoris and a dampening sensation between her legs.

Walking into the shed she stripped off her clothes, took out her mobile and dialled the home phone. When Jon answered she made her voice quiver; she was renowned for her fear of rodents.

'Darling, I went into the shed for the pruning shears and saw a mouse. I am standing on the paint tins at the back and I'm too scared to move!'

'I'll be right there,' Jon said, years of practical experience managing to keep him from making the mistake of laughing… but only just!

Susan hung up, drawing the forsythia branches up her legs and across her belly with a huge grin on her face.

She could hear Jon approaching and then he flung open the door saying, 'How is the mouse supposed to have a chance to escape when the shed door is…' He stopped short when he saw the look on her face and her nakedness draped with branches of yellow blossoms.

'Get your clothes off and get down on your knees or you'll never find out what you're missing!'

Jon had his trousers down around his knees by the end of her sentence. His penis was already stirring in anticipation. Susan flicked it gently with one of the flimsier branches. His cock twitched in response. He puddled his clothes on the floor and kneeled on them, looking up at Susan to indicate his readiness. This was all the encouragement she needed; she picked up a small selection of branches and stood at his side; drawing them from his rounded bum to his straining shoulders. She spent a while flicking them against that gorgeous ass of his, each impact harder than the last, until it reddened enough to match the flush on his chest and face. Next she ran the blossom-laden branches up each leg, making sure to brush against his scrotum. His arms trembled and his breath hissed.

Susan could feel her clit twitching and her labia swelling with arousal. Moving to stand in front of Jon, she spread her

22

legs and ran her hand down over her belly, curving her fingers into her pussy and bringing them back up to stroke her nub of pleasure.

His eyes hooded with lust and he murmured, 'do it Susan, do it'.

Too close to the edge and unwilling to stop just to tease him further, she rubbed herself frantically to a shuddering climax, much to Jon's delight. He had told her many times how much of a turn on it was to watch her bring herself off. In his opinion, watching the utter abandon of a truly liberated woman was pleasure in itself.

After she had recovered, Susan turned to assisting with Jon's gratification. Aware she was onto a good thing, she pulled the forsythia branches up her own legs, making sure the blossoms brushed past her wet lips, coating them in some of her own lubrication before sweeping them past his face.

Jon was sitting back on his heels, greedily watching her, his penis engorged and rising up to thump him in the stomach from time to time. This spurred her on and she rubbed herself, smearing moisture onto her finger tips and ran this around her nipples. They stood upright, shining with their glossy coating and sending tingles directly down to her already aching clit.

Jon settled into a sitting position and reached up to touch her. He moved his palms in a sweeping upward motion along the inside of her thighs and Susan spread her legs to invite and accommodate his wet mouth. He dipped his tongue in and out of her moistness and began gently stroking her clit with his fingers. Before long Susan's hips were rhythmically grinding down onto the contact. Susan turned and leaned against the old chest of drawers and then mewled with displeasure when he stopped playing with her in order to stand up. Upright, he pressed against her, reaching round to slide his fingers into her wet hole and she

23

began to buck her ass against his hardness. Placing his hands on her hips, he leaned away enough to bend his knees and position himself so his cock slid between her legs. Gently, ever so gently, he rocked back and forth purposefully stroking her clit with his hard cock. Then he leaned against her, cock still hot against her labia and began to kiss the back of her neck until she tilted her ass up and against his stomach, inviting his entry into her wet centre. Knowing she was ready and, unable to contain himself, he plunged into her in one smooth stroke. Susan thrust back and forth, riding his cock and the pressure of his fingers, which were once again on her clit, with his other hand wrapped round her breast, clinging onto her bucking hips with the pressure of his own. It seemed an eternity and simultaneously only seconds before they were both joyously climaxing.

Today she had woken alone, his pillow still warm, to find a note on the breakfast bar. The morning light had slanted through the partially open blinds casting shadows on the paper. In her haste to move to better light, she nearly tripped over their cat, Taz, who was winding herself around her legs.

'See you at the Tazwell barn, 12 o'clock, love you'. He had drawn the note instead of writing it, leaving her a rough sketch of eyes, a U, @, their cat beside a well, a barn and a clock with hands poised at 12, a heart and a U. She smiled to herself at his unique form of communication, this was exactly what kept her so fired up about him, little things like the fact that he had taken the time to do more than just write a note; they'd been together ten years now, these efforts kept her besotted. She finished her morning ablutions, then readied herself for work, remembering to put her walking boots and a change of clothes in the car, so she could change and go straight to the woods from work.

24

She drove as fast the traffic would allow, marvelling at how rush hour seemed to start earlier every year. The weak spring sunshine and warming air seemed to bring everyone out of winter hibernation and, like the tree buds, they all seemed to be bursting with good cheer. It wasn't very often queues of traffic would part to allow her entry to the main roundabout but today seemed to be an exception! Perhaps it was the fact that she was brimming with happiness that cast a happy glow over everything, even the snarls of vehicles which would normally annoy her for the duration of the journey.

She could see the barn roof as she turned into the lane. She parked and walked to the veranda that had been built onto the front of the barn: now a trendy coffee shop which sold home-made baked goods, preserves and cider. Jon stepped away from the post he'd been leaning on and gave her a soft open kiss. Looking into his eyes, Susan could feel a thrill run through her ending with a reflexive throb in her clit. Susan led the way behind the Tazwell Barn to the woods with Jon following a half step behind, his hand on the small of her back. The sunlight dappled through the tree branches, lighting up the soft green of the new leaves. The musty smell of the damp bark and loamy smell of the rich soil combined with Jon's presence stimulated her deep inside where her basest instincts simmered; sending tendrils of lust flicking down her belly. Hand in hand, they meandered along the path until Susan stumbled when distracted by a particularly noisy pair of courting pigeons. Clutching onto Jon's hand stopped her from sprawling face first onto the path. Giggling, she let Jon lower her to the ground. As she settled herself, he turned his back to her and plucked something off a tree.

'Look, it matches the colour of your eyes' he said holding up a small sycamore leaf which had somehow lasted the winter attached to the tree and was still displaying its autumnal colours. The veins were wrapped in a parchment of mottled soft brown highlighted with glowing ambers and bright yellowy orange.

He took out his wallet and placed the leaf between the two halves, gently closing it before tucking it in his front pocket. He sat down beside her, leaning over for a kiss. Susan eagerly met him halfway and they stayed this way, until her nipples had hardened from the sensation of their teeth nibbling each other's lips, ears and necks.

She began squirming, trying to get her hands up the front of her coat to get to her bra clasp and tantalise him by freeing her breasts. With any luck he would be enticed into placing his hot mouth over her nipples, sucking them deeply.

'Don't,' he said and, shocked, she opened her eyes. Finger on his lips and already halfway to standing upright, he grasped her with his other hand and drew her up beside him. Then she heard it too, voices that were moving closer. They stood there; feeling vaguely like guilty teenagers until the group had passed, casting them sideways glances and each other knowing grins as they went. Susan threw her arms around Jon's neck and he gripped her hips, walking her backwards until she was stopped by a tree.

Sliding his hands up under her coat and shirt, he unclasped her bra, lifted her garments and made her melt with his mouth. She ran her hand down the inside of his waistband, gripping his hard cock and gently squeezing before curving her hand down and around the base of his tightening balls. She spent some time stroking her fingers from the tip of his rectum to the end of his balls, knowing from experience the pleasure this gave Jon.

26

Then they undid each other's zippers, frantic and clumsy in their haste. He pushed his boxers down to his knees and pulled her thong to one side, the friction of the gusset an unexpected pleasure. The bark of the tree gripped her and offered support when he lifted her up onto his throbbing penis. He filled her in one smooth motion, the position they were in directed the pressure of his entry directly onto her C-Spot, making her come with the second stroke. He stopped then, allowing the clenching and relaxing of her muscles to drive him through his own climax.

They stayed this way, mouths open against each other, until they recovered enough for Susan to realise that her coat was mostly up above her shoulders and head, her bare ass resting on the bark and for Jon to become aware of his legs trembling. Jon eased Susan down to a standing position so they could both adjust their clothing before someone came along the path.

'I'm starving! Lets stop at the Tazwell for some treats to eat in the garden. I want to admire the neatly trimmed forsythia,' Jon winked mischievously, before grabbing her hand and planting a kiss on it.

'Darling woman of mine, you make my soul sing.'

Educating Emma
by Kristina Wright

Art is my passion, my reason for living. I hold degrees in art and psychology and I have been teaching at the School of Contemporary Arts for three years. Art is my calling, but psychology allows me to look into people's souls and discover their deepest desires – and how to fulfil them.

I was halfway through a promising spring semester with a gifted group of young freshmen, all girls and one uninspired boy. They were awe-struck by me, though I wasn't much older than them, and one girl in particular caught my attention.

Emma was a natural beauty, fresh-faced and truly innocent, with none of the artifice the other girls possessed. She wore her dark hair long and her face was delicate and fine-boned, requiring no make-up to enhance her flawlessness. She was also a gifted artist, capturing colour and light in such vivid detail as to render it nearly photographic.

I was standing behind her one afternoon, studying her sketches from a previous class. Her hair smelled fresh and clean and, unlike the other girls who preferred low-slung jeans and belly-baring T-shirts, she wore a simple pink cotton dress and sandals. She was innocence incarnate and I felt a little rush of power, knowing that the young woman would soon be writhing in naked, lustful abandon before her classmates – and her boyfriend.

The boyfriend, a sad-looking young man named Danny, chose that moment to interrupt my daydream.

'Uh... Ms Wentworth... I was, like, wondering – '

I sighed. 'What *is* it, Danny?'

'Um, I kind of need to leave early because I have to see my allergist.'

The boy was unworthy of such a beautiful, luscious creature as Emma. She, unfortunately, didn't seem to realise it. She smiled at him, completely enamoured by his pimply skin and scrawny body. I didn't understand the attraction. I'd heard the other girls talk about the couple and how they hadn't yet slept together because Danny couldn't get up the nerve to entice her into bed. It didn't surprise me. It was unlikely Danny would ever have sex unless some woman took pity on him and made the first move. Emma, lovely and sensual as she was, wasn't going to be that woman.

'Today's class is of the utmost importance,' I said with disdain. 'I really must insist you stay for the duration as missing this class could seriously impact your grade and your continued enrolment in the program.'

'Well, uh, I... I'll stay. I'll just be late or maybe I can call at the break and reschedule or something...'

I left him babbling and walked to the front of the class.

'As some of you who have taken previous classes with me know, this is the point in the semester when we turn our attention to live model drawing.'

There were a few hushed giggles among the girls.

'For this class, you're not required to draw, but simply to observe and, perhaps, participate. Observation, of course, is the artist's greatest asset, far more important than any brush or canvas. Participation is the artist transcending the art to become performance art. Observe and learn.'

As I finished speaking, the door to the classroom opened and two young men entered. Both were dressed in jeans and white T-shirts, and I knew from previous experience that neither was wearing underwear.

'We'll begin by studying the male form,' I said. 'As I'm sure you will agree, Carlos and Ian are fine examples.'

I glanced pointedly at Danny, who blushed uncomfortably. In contrast, Emma glowed with excitement.

'Gentlemen,' I said, gesturing to the centre of the room. 'Please undress.'

Carlos quickly stripped off his T-shirt, revealing broad shoulders and rock hard abs. My pulse quickened as he unsnapped his jeans. Ian followed suit and, in a few short moments, both men were gloriously naked. I admired their bodies only cursorily, more interested in Emma's response. She looked back and forth at the two men, as if comparing them, her gaze lingering on their long, thick cocks. I'd chosen the men for their endowments as well as for the beautiful contrast between Carlos's olive complexion and Ian's fair one. Their bodies were different as any two bodies will be and it was this I wanted to impress upon my students.

'Carlos, if you would be so kind as to stroke yourself to erection,' I said. 'Students, please make note of the differences in shape and colour between a flaccid penis and an aroused one.'

Carlos fisted his cock as requested, until it was hard and thick. I could hear the appreciative gasps of the girls in the room, including Emma. I smiled.

'Now you, Ian. Please show the students how the male form can differ, even in arousal.'

Ian followed Carlos's lead, bringing his cock to its full, erect glory.

'They're so gay.'

31

It was barely a whisper, meant only for Emma's ears, but I heard it.

'What did you say, Danny?' I asked the question so sharply that all eyes turned to me, which was no small feat considering there were two beautiful, naked men in the room. 'Do you care to repeat that comment for the rest of us?'

Danny blushed. 'Um, no Ms Wentworth.'

I tapped my stiletto heel on the concrete floor. 'No? You don't want to announce to the entire class that you think our invited guests are gay? Well, I was going to ask for a volunteer to demonstrate the many interesting variations in the human body, but I think your rude, disrespectful comment has earned you the job.'

Miserably, Danny stood and went to the centre of the room. He was flanked by two impressive, naked men and ringed by a group of his female peers who didn't seem to know whether to laugh or take the whole thing seriously.

'Undress, Danny,' I commanded.

'Ma'am?'

I sighed impatiently. 'In order for us to compare the anatomies of male bodies, we must actually *see* the male bodies.'

This raised a twitter of girlish laughter

'I can't... I mean... c'mon, Ms Wentworth,' Danny whined.

'I told you this class was important to your grade,' I said. 'I emphasised it quite succinctly, yet you've chosen to disrupt the class, insult our guests and push my patience to the edge.'

'I'm sorry.'

I went on as if I hadn't heard him. 'You have two choices. You may undress and serve as a model for the class or you may leave now and fail the semester.'

32

Danny was on scholarship and a failing grade would mean losing his financial support. I was betting he would stay and I was right.

He began to undress and I had to look away because the sight of him stripping off his baggy yellow underwear was too sad for words. He stood between Carlos and Ian, covering his genitals and looking horrified by his predicament.

'Good. Now demonstrate how your – um, attributes – differ from Carlos and Ian's by arousing yourself.'

Danny shook his head, as if it was a question. I glanced at Emma, who stared at Danny as if she'd never seen him before. Her sexuality all but oozed from her pores and it made me sick to think of her giving herself to Danny. She deserved so much more than anything he could do for her.

Danny opened his mouth as if to protest, but then closed it just as quickly. He quickly stroked his penis, but it simply refused to get hard.

'Never mind,' I snapped. I scanned the other students. 'Now, as you can see, the human male form comes in many shapes – and sizes.' I grimaced faintly as I stared at Danny's puny penis, ignoring the giggles as I went on. 'The female form, by comparison, has its own peaks and valleys, slopes and shadows. Would anyone care to volunteer?'

I had only one young woman in mind to undress, so I ignored the two or three hesitant hands that went up and turned my attention to Emma. 'Emma, you seem to be the most comfortably dressed, perhaps you'd care to volunteer since your body won't be marred by unsightly clothing marks?'

I'd expected her to resist, but she surprised me. 'Of course, Ms Wentworth.'

I heard a grunt of protest from Danny, but I ignored it. This was what I had hoped for and it was working out exactly as I had imagined.

Emma stood beside Carlos, a faint blush in her youthful cheeks. She quickly removed her dress, revealing full, luscious, bra-less breasts and sheer pink panties.

'Beautiful,' I breathed. 'Simply stunning.'

Danny looked around Carlos to see his girlfriend. His gaze wandered down her body, pausing briefly at her large breasts before lingering on the dark triangle of pubic hair visible through her panties. He stared like a starving man and I detected the barest twitch of interest in his slug-like penis.

'Danny, are you getting an erection standing between two well-endowed naked men?' I asked sharply.

The boy positively glared at me. 'No! I'm looking at Emma!'

'Ogling women is not a part of this class, Danny. How would you like it if Emma stared at you?'

Danny's head drooped.

'Emma, would you please remove your panties and give them to Danny?' I said, gently.

Emma didn't hesitate. The wispy panties came off and she held them out to Danny, who stared at the sheer fabric as if it was a snake.

'Put Emma's panties on, please.'

'No!'

I was growing tired of Danny's rebellion. 'You are wasting our time. If you wish to stare at Emma as if she were here for your own personal pleasure, than you will have to endure the same sexist treatment. Put the panties *on.*'

Danny took the panties from Emma and put them on, his half-hard penis a sad lump for the entire class to see.

The girls giggled and pointed, making hushed comments about Danny's small penis compared to that of the two men.

'Ian, would you and Danny please move aside?'

'Yes, ma'am.' Ian took Danny's arm and pulled him next to me, the two looking like a before-and-after set of pictures.

'Carlos, please take Emma in your arms to demonstrate the subtleties of skin colour and muscle tone.'

Carlos held his hand out to Emma. For the first time, Emma hesitated. I could see the flush in her cheeks and knew it was at least as much from excitement as it was from embarrassment. She looked to Danny, her expression pleading. The coward dropped his gaze and Emma looked to me instead.

'It's all right, Emma,' I said softly. 'You'll enjoy this, I promise.'

She smiled, seemingly comforted. 'OK, Ms Wentworth.'

'Good. Now Carlos, if you will manoeuvre Emma to show the other students how the human form can be manipulated for artistic purposes.'

I was careful to emphasise the word 'artistic.' I didn't want Emma to think this was anything but an assignment in live model studies.

Carlos wrapped his arms around Emma's waist from behind, so that his powerful forearms supported her heavy breasts. There were oohs from the other girls, no doubt because they could imagine what it would be like to be held by Carlos, to have his thick penis nestling between the cheeks of their asses.

Emma gasped, no doubt feeling that very thing. At first I thought she might pull away, but she only settled deeper into Carlos's arms – and against his cock.

'Good. As you can see, Emma's smooth, porcelain skin provides a very exciting contrast to the ripples of Carlos's muscles and his olive complexion,' I said. 'Can you imagine what a challenge it would be to capture such contrasts on canvas without minimizing either's natural beauty?'

A few girls nodded, the rest were mesmerized by the image before them.

I pulled Emma's stool to the centre of the room. 'Why don't you sit down, Carlos? Then you can support Emma more easily.'

Carlos sat, his erection appearing longer and thicker from having been pressed against Emma's tight bottom, and once again extended his hand to the young woman. She took it without hesitation and nestled between Carlos's legs, facing the class.

'Excellent. Would place your arms behind you so we may note the curves of your body in comparison to the angles of Carlos's shoulders and thighs?'

Emma did as I requested, her eyes going wide as her hands made contact with Carlos's hard cock. This position thrust her breasts forward and her hard, pink nipples presented a delectable sight. With a nod from me, Carlos trailed his hands down the front of her chest until he gently cupped her breasts in his large, tanned hands.

The young girl gasped, but she didn't pull away. It seemed, in fact, as if she were doing something behind her back. I smirked. The little minx was stroking Carlos's cock, hoping no one would notice.

Carlos began rolling her nipples between his fingers, tugging and twisting them until Emma began squirming and moaning.

'Very nice,' I murmured.

I glanced at Danny, who stared at the scene with a mixture of anger and envy. His erection poked from the top of Emma's panties, threatening to rip the thin fabric. He realised I was looking at him and started toward the embracing couple as if he intended to pull Emma away.

'Ian, would you please restrain Danny? I'm afraid he can't control himself.'

Ian grabbed a resisting Danny and pulled his arms behind his back, mirroring Emma's pose. 'Watch it, little boy. Don't forget, I'm gay. I might decide to fuck you if you don't play nice.'

The girl closest to me said, 'He might like that.'

Several girls nodded in agreement. Danny immediately stopped struggling and stood there quietly in his girlfriend's panties, watching her being fondled by another man.

'Good, Danny,' I soothed. 'I think you'll appreciate the next part of this presentation.'

Carlos was still pinching and squeezing Emma's nipples and she made no attempt to pull away. In fact, she rested her head on Carlos's shoulder, thrusting her breasts more fully into his hands.

'Oh, I wish that was me,' one of the girls said. 'You love it, don't you, Emma?'

Emma nodded, lost in sensation.

When I realised Emma couldn't take it any longer, I nodded to Carlos. 'Put her on your lap.'

He easily lifted the girl onto his lap so that her legs were on the outside of his and she was spread open. A collective gasp went up from the class at the image they presented: Emma straddling Carlos so that her pink, glistening pussy was poised just above his massive erection.

'Now, ladies, this is the moment where life becomes art. Imagine how you would capture such a scene, what strokes you would use, what colours you would blend to achieve your desired effect,' I instructed softly. 'Carlos, you may do whatever you feel would be most effective in demonstrating this lesson.'

Around the room, a dozen pairs of eyes were riveted on the two naked forms in front of us. We held our collective breaths while Emma shifted impatiently, anxious for what only Carlos could give her.

'Please,' Emma whispered. 'Please.'

Carlos reached around her narrow waist and stroked the delicate folds of her engorged pussy. Her eyes fluttered closed as she gasped, pushing against Carlos's exploring fingers. He slid first one, then two, thick digits between her tender folds and she moaned.

Next to me, Ian said, 'Don't you wish that was you, little guy? Don't you wish you were playing with your girl's puss right now?'

Danny whimpered pathetically and I almost felt sorry for him.

I expected Carlos to substitute his throbbing erection for the fingers in Emma's pussy, but the horny young girl surprised me. She reached down between her spread thighs and stroked the thick cock that was so close to her pussy.

'Please,' she said again. 'I need this. Please.'

Carlos obeyed the minx's wishes and covered her hand with his. Together, they guided his cock into her juicy cunt, stretching the lips wide with the meaty head. She gasped and grunted, her large breasts heaving, as she took him inside her. With excruciating slowness, Carlos's cock slid into her inch by impressive inch, until she could accommodate no more.

With his arms under her thighs for support, Carlos spread her wide on his cock for the entire class to see. He then lifted her up, his cock emerging from her cunt, glistening with the evidence of her arousal. The girls gasped appreciatively and I knew every pussy in the room was wet with desire, including my own.

With incredible restraint, Carlos carefully and slowly lowered Emma back onto his cock until she was once again impaled. Sweat glistened on his brow and I knew he was dying to fuck the girl hard, fuck her like no man had ever fucked such a beauty.

Emma cupped and kneaded her own breasts, her head thrown back against Carlos's shoulder as she moaned, 'More, more!'

Carlos began fucking the girl hard, raising and lowering her on his cock until she writhed and moaned. She clutched at her own body, twisting her nipples, scratching her thighs, and gyrating her cunt on the thick cock inside her. She was no longer a dedicated young art student; she was a wanton beauty, a sex-hungry slut.

'I'm going to come!' she screamed, announcing her impending orgasm to the room. 'Fuck me, fuck me hard!'

'Emma!' The name sounded as if it was ripped painfully from Danny's throat. 'What are you doing?'

She looked at him, through him, so caught up in the sensations of her body she could barely seem to focus. 'I'm getting fucked, Danny. I'm getting fucked,' she gasped.

Carlos drove his cock up into her with such force the stool rocked. He held her in his powerful arms and fucked her senseless, groaning in masculine desire. Danny struggled in Ian's powerful arms, whimpering pitifully.

'Watch her get fucked, Danny,' I taunted the boy. 'See how she loves his big cock inside her? You can't do that for her.'

Two things happened almost simultaneously: Carlos came, deep inside Emma's tight cunt and Danny came, in Emma's pretty pink panties. Both men groaned, but only Carlos had the satisfaction of feeling Emma's wet cunt surround him as she squeezed his cock in post-orgasmic bliss. He held her to him as he slowly softened and slipped free of her beautiful body, leaving a trail of glistening wetness behind.

The pair cuddled on the stool as the class applauded.

'That was beautiful, simply beautiful,' I said. I looked at Danny, who was staring in misery at the wet spot his over-excited dick had left on Emma's panties. 'Don't you agree this was a beautiful piece of performance art, Danny?'

Danny looked at me, torn between humiliation and a need for approval. 'Um, yeah, I can see that.'

I shook my head, disgusted with Danny and determined to get him thrown out of the art program. I met Emma's gaze from across the room and she smiled radiantly, mouthing two simple words.

'Thank you.'

Heels, Stockings, Girdle, Bra, Face
by Jeremy Edwards

I couldn't understand why you suggested we meet tonight at the empty condo that your sister is in the middle of renovating. You said you wanted to give me a 'tour'. Now that I've arrived, I understand what kind of tour you meant. A tour of you, not the condo. The condo is just a convenient, distraction-free setting – with a big-ass air conditioner in the middle of the floor. Nice. But I shouldn't scoff. With you standing dramatically atop it in your lingerie, the air conditioner in the middle of the floor *is* nice.

Heels

I'll start with the least important. And, since you *will* insist on standing atop an out-of-commission air conditioner, the first stratum of your accoutrements to meet my eye.

Those black heels.

I call them 'heels', but in actuality they are entire shoes. You, on the other hand, call them *stilettos*.

I'm not the kind of guy to over-glamorize heels. Women can be sexy as all get-out without them – barefoot, for example. I don't think anyone should feel pressured to wear heels, if they're impractical or uncomfortable or bad for their feet.

But if you feel like wearing them, then far be it from me to argue. Far be it from me, in fact, to resist ogling them on you. Yes, I admit I very much like the way they position the erotic structure of your sassy feet. The glossy black texture is the perfect trim for your stockings. I do hope, by the way, that the 'leather' is synthetic; I want you to be the only animal in those shoes. Rrrrr!

You've explained that they are too high, technically, to qualify as 'fuck-me' heels. I maintain that any heel worn by you, standing in lingerie on an air conditioner, is a 'fuck-me' heel. And I intend to prove it.

My favorite thing about these shoes is how you react when I slip a finger inside one of them and tickle your arch, with great delicacy, through the thin thickness of your stocking. You adore being gently tickled; you press your foot against my finger, wedging it tightly and inviting more sensuous strokes, while your musical giggles rain down from far above. I am looking forward to tickling your other places as well. You have so many places.

I imagine following you across a kitchen floor, as your heels go *click click click click*. You deliberately dead-end against the refrigerator, and I come to a stop with cushy precision, pressed against your own end, which is anything but dead. As I manage to give your ass a series of fabric caresses with my trouser front, I am conscious of the heels that elevate your rear cheeks to a perfect fondling height.

Of course, at the moment, since you're posed atop an air conditioner, your behind is out of reach. It is a goal I shall later attain. For the moment, though, I caress your ankles.

You can't give much lateral motion to your feet in these stilettos, but I can detect your erotic tension throbbing inside the shoes. My titillations travel silently, by means of your nervous system, up your legs to your pussy, whence

42

sexual signals pulsate back down the stocking highway to your blushing feet. It arouses me to feel your passion burn against my fingers, way down here in your sexy shoes.

Though you're standing on an air conditioner, I visualize you in a comfortable seat in a shoe department, and I visualize myself as the shoe salesman. I am fitting you for these black heels, easily coaxing the right shoe onto your foot, while you smile at me. Your foot fits the shoe like my cock fits your cunt – the tightness is pleasant but not excessively constraining, the sensation of flesh against the comfortable inner walls is luxurious, and sensuous wiggling is most encouraged. I hold your foot, in the shoe, in my hand, and gently work your heel in my palm, testing you for snugness.

As I return from this daydream, I smell woman in the air, and it is then that I notice that you have no panties on beneath your open bottom girdle, and that I have a clear view.

Stockings

Your bare legs are deliciously smooth, but when you encase them in these black stockings they become impossibly smooth. Physicists tell us that a body in motion will, in the absence of friction, travel forever. This is what your legs now promise me – an infinite journey. Accordingly, they seem to stretch on endlessly, seen from my vantage point below. And yet, there is a clear place where the stockings end, and the legs become legs no more, but skin-fresh upper thighs. Above the dark stocking tops, I know we're in a region that's close enough to your pussy to have elements of its flavour – just as the air within a few miles of the ocean has an unmistakable seaside tang.

Your legs, in these stockings, appear like twin columns, a portico that proclaims the entrance to some hallowed place. I don't think I need to elaborate on this. Suffice it to say that, as I stand at the base of your air conditioner mountain, I feel like I'm looking up at a glorious secular temple – a library, an observatory, or a museum. Then I smell your fragrance again, and suddenly I'm more inclined to compare you to a fine restaurant. I'm eager to park and claim my reservation.

But I feel like I could stroke your legs all night, while they remain in these stockings. The nylon makes an almost-inaudible hum against my fingers. (Is this what a zither sounds like? A gentle 'Zzzzz'? It ought to be.) As I stroke up and down, up and down your leg, my cock feels like you are stroking up and down, up and down, its length. Do you notice how I begin to dance in place as I pet you? That's my arousal dancing through me, my dear, as you knew it would when you dressed yourself in these impossibly-smooth stockings that point me to your cunt. I can travel up whichever leg I like – they both lead to the same place. (All roads lead to Rome.)

Fabric and flesh – a contrast of both textures and colours. Your skin happens to be pale, so the contrast lies in the interplay of your white thighs and your black stockings. The nylon is synthetic, and you, of course, are deliciously organic – another contrast. The stockings have a uniform hue and tone that do not change, whereas your upper thighs grow slightly pinker as our situation arouses you, and their texture becomes, in places, slightly slick with a discreet trickle of lubrication from above. Yes, I can see them from here, places on the private side of your picture-frame of thighs where the light sparkles just so, dancing with your stickiness in a rhythm that I mimic with my gentle samba of male horniness.

I'm at the point where I feel the compulsion to take further action. I can reach your stocking-tops and the garter clips that attach them to your girdle, and I unfasten each clip, caressing you behind your knees all the while. Then I peel you like a fruit, slithering each stocking down and following its progress with a trail of kisses along and around the corresponding leg. The sudden nakedness of each leg shouts at me – to see them uncovered feels, at this moment, more boldly carnal and explicit than looking straight into your pussy lips on a typical Friday night.

It's not practical to remove your shoes, so I leave the stockings bunched around your ankles. You look so happily exposed now, my smiling, bare-legged, bunched-stocking girl. Oh, how I'm going to fuck you.

Girdle

When you told me about the garment you'd purchased, my tongue was probably hanging out in anticipation. Red silk (PANTONE 192) all over your ass . . . peekaboo laces to commemorate where your butt cheeks meet . . . the hem open like the bell of a trumpet, so that your pussy can feel the delight of every warm breeze and invite wandering fingers (either yours or mine, depending on whose are handy). What more could I ask for from an article of lingerie?

Well, I could ask that you save it for a special occasion – which you did. I could ask that you invite me to inaugurate it with you – which you have. Mine shall be the first fingertips that stroke the silk across your firm cheeks and sturdy mound. Mine shall be the first thumbs that fumble with its laces, in my haste to unwrap you. Mine shall be the first drop of pre-cum that streaks across the smooth feminine fabric, while I press myself against you.

The girdle fits you almost like gym shorts, so tight against your tight but womanly but tight but feminine little ass. It grips you like I want to. Now I climb onto the air conditioner with you to do so. Here at your level, I will squeeze your cushion in its silk pillowcase, unthread its laces and lick across the pillowy flesh in broad, sensuous strokes . . . left cheek, then right cheek, etc. You get the idea.

Ah, but before I do that, I must take advantage of the open girdle's opening. Your legs part and my face enters the cosy place within your silken tepee. While you stand open for me in your open bottom girdle, I tongue the parts of you that panties would have concealed. I will make you so glad you're not wearing panties, darling. Perhaps you'll talk to me about the advantages of going without panties while I lick and lick you, explaining to me between heavy breaths how what I'm doing and what you're feeling make a strong case for the panty-free approach to lingerie.

Just the name 'open bottom girdle' makes me drool. These words seem to positively proclaim your interest in having me visit pleasure upon your feminine regions. 'Open bar' means unlimited drinks. 'Open road' means limitless horizons. 'Open door' means opportunities await within; no need to knock. And 'open bottom girdle' means my head between your thighs. This garment was made for you . . . for us.

Its hem feels so delicate between my fingers. Yet I am clutching it firmly, like I might hold onto the corners of waxed paper while I devour a many-layered sandwich. I am about to make a meal of you, and you're even generating your own sweet condiment. I can literally taste your excitement.

It feels intimate and joyfully *secret* to know that the orgasm you're having is happening inside your girdle. I'm right in there with you, dancing with your cunt, miles above your distant heels, which rock sensuously as you writhe. I love feeling like an insider, where female orgasms are concerned. I could stay in here all day, lips to your lips, listening to your thighs reverberate with pleasure as they clamp against my ears.

46

I feel an extra spasm jolt through your thighs as my fingertips once again find the space between the laces on your ass. It's as if there's a direct erotic line from your ass crack to your clit, an express train of pleasure that makes my caress at your rear trigger juicy ecstasy in my face, quicker than lightning.

Bra

I've never thought of myself as a 'breast man'. But there are breasts and there are breasts. Anyway, it's the woman behind the breasts that really makes a pair of breasts exciting. In this instance, the breasts are modest in size, aesthetic in curvature, and flirtatious in attitude. And the woman behind them is . . . you. If clutching these breasts will make pleasure course through your sweet little body, then I am all about clutching these breasts. And how could I resist, for that matter? They fit perfectly in my hands. They have a fresh, gentle, fleshy fragrance. And they're displayed in a classic black lace bra.

Whoever figured out that black lace sets off white breasts deserves the applause of the generations. The opaque leaves play across the hazy, breast-flesh background like blue designs on white china. It drives me wild to know that the background of the lace design is, in fact, your soft, round flesh, the flesh of a zone so erogenous that my merest touch or tickle makes fruit juice moisten your sex lips. And when I touch a nipple, it's like I've pressed a button that sends you rocketing into feminine joys that are impossible to conceive. I can't wait to be inside you, clutching you from ass to shoulders, these lace-wrapped breasts pushing themselves against me like puppies, your head thrown back as if all your being were consumed in a nurturing bath of pleasure.

It's lewdly delicious that you would leave your cunt exposed in an open bottom girdle while modestly enshrouding your breasts in a lace brassiere. I think about this as I trace the elegant lace leaves, curly stems, that little bud . . . Oh! my mistake. It was a female nipple, not a lingerie bud, and you're clutching my elbow for support because the pleasure of being touched there has made you almost unable to stand on your fuck-me-till-I-can't-stand-up heels. Before the night is over, we'll climb down from this air conditioner and head for the futon, so you can properly fall on your ass with delight when I touch you certain places. There's a feather duster somewhere around here, and I can already visualize the way you'll grind your bottom into the futon if I chance to brush inside that open girdle with the hint of a feather. By then, I think we'll have to remove the delicate bra, because your precious nipples will be hungering for my kisses while your wild behind squirms against the bed.

As I undo your bra clasps and the lace garment falls far below, beyond the air conditioner, your naked breasts present themselves to me. 'Present' is an apt verb, because I feel like I'm being handed twin presents, i.e. nouns, gifts from your beauty to my appetite. All the physical softness that is woman is distilled into these beautiful, round attributes, so precious that you wrapped them up in fancy lace until I was ready to enjoy them. Your feet have enticed me, your legs have engaged me, your behind, as always, has lured me and your pussy has already, for the first but not last time tonight, enfolded me. But there's one thing that your breasts offer which these other attributes do not – proximity to your face. It's a special kind of bliss to make love to your breasts with my kisses and squeezes and see your face looking down on me, transfixed by the sensations I'm bestowing.

Face

I think the thing that impresses me the most about your face, when I'm sculpting your body with erotic touches, is its air of concentration. It's as if you're not only experiencing but also studying every sensation, memorising each tiny bubble of pleasure and every detail of the orgasms big and small, as if you were going to be tested on them later. I know that you live your life so as to get the most out of things – savouring each morsel of food, sensuously swirling every drop of wine around your mouth, giving the striking things you find in the natural and artistic world that extra moment of attention, so as to thoroughly milk their beauty into your soul. And this is also how you approach sex. You are completely aware of the height, breadth, depth, shape, texture, colour, density, specific gravity, molecular weight and favourite ice cream flavour of each sexual sensation, and your extraordinary gift for concentration allows you, paradoxically, to swallow each moment of ecstasy in one piece and yet taste every ingredient before it has vanished.

It blows my mind that it's *my* touches, *my* erotic contact, and *my* desire that you devote all this attention to. Nobody else has ever paid the level of attention to anything of mine that you give to every taste of my lips or stroke of my fingers. As you clutch my cock, I feel like you're reading a novel's worth of detail in every centimetre of my flesh. I can see it in your eyes, those focused, impossibly-deep eyes, which reflect all my lust, all my love, and a richness of sensation that dwarfs my own self-awareness.

The expression in your face now comprises the frank provocativeness of your shoes, the sleek seductiveness of your stockings, the pussy-bare willingness of your girdle, and the demure ripeness of your bra. All of that, and so much more. An immediately-nearby mirror of my passion, and an infinitely-deep window into your own.

We've finally cleared your ankles of the stockings and your feet of the stilettos, and I'm inside you now, with your legs wrapped around me. Your face is as close to mine as it could be without becoming invisible to me. Sensuality creeps outward from your mouth, across all your other features, as your lips form the beginnings of phrases such as 'Oh my God' and 'Fuck me.' You don't have to actually say them for me to know what you're feeling. I'm feeling it, too, after all. As you scream an orgasm into my face I lose myself in a stand-up explosion of froth from my tip into your core, a roomful of lingerie seems to spin around me. From atop a retired air conditioner, the whole world smells like your pleasure, and I appreciate more than ever why you chose every detail so carefully, to orchestrate this moment so flawlessly. In dressing yourself, you have in fact dressed an occasion, an event – and, in the timeless world of ecstasy, an eternity. Well done.

'Do You Trust Me?'
by Sommer Marsden

'May I use that for a minute?'

I turned to hand over the corkscrew. Warm hazel eyes met my gaze. Dark hair, just a little too long. It fell boyishly over his forehead. I tracked the edge of his jaw with my eyes, took in the perfectly shaped mouth. Red lips. Not too red, just red enough to make me wonder what it would be like to kiss them.

'May I?' he asked again with a smile.

I realised I was still holding the corkscrew out. Offering it up but not letting it go. I shrugged, tried to cover with a laugh. I released the tool into his broad palm and wondered for a split second if that palm was soft or calloused. What it would feel like sliding under my skirt and along my stockings. 'Sure, sorry. Maybe I shouldn't have this glass after all.'

'Oh, I don't know about that. I think you just became a little absorbed for a moment. It happens to the best of us.' He flashed that smile again and I felt a warmth start low in my belly. I liked his smile very much.

'I was. Just a little.' I shrugged. No reason to lie, I had been obvious enough from the get-go.

'Well, my ego would prefer it if you said a lot, but I will take a little and be happy with it.' He began to uncork the bottle of Chablis he was holding. 'Not for me,' he explained. 'I prefer red. I was told someone with muscles needed to open a fresh bottle. Not that I'm riddled with them, mind you. A respectable amount, though.'

I took this as an invitation to scope out his muscles, so I did just that. He didn't have the over-inflated look of a gym rat, but a respectable amount was not an understatement. Broad shoulders that hinted at strength. His arms, cut just enough that the contours showed through the cotton Henley he was wearing. It looked soft, too, that shirt. I repressed the urge to run my hands along the swells and dips cloaked in frequently washed cotton.

'Still a little absorbed?' he laughed as the cork broke free with a jubilant *pop!*

'No.' I took a sip of my wine and smiled. 'A lot.'

He let out a laugh and the hair on the back of my neck stirred with appreciation of the sound. He grabbed his chest and sighed. 'It does an ego good to hear it. I'm Eric.'

He took my hand before I could offer it. He didn't shake. He just squeezed it gently. Another stirring of baby fine hair, this time up my arms.

'Ashling. Ash to most.' He hadn't let my hand go and I didn't try to remove it. I liked the feel of his warm skin surrounding mine.

Eric leaned in close and whispered. 'I like your dress. Very deceptive.'

I glanced down as if I had never seen the dress. It was my favourite. Snug without being too tight. The front cut so that it fell just below my collar bones. Very modest. But the back. Well, there was no back. From behind my neck where the dress buttoned to the small of my back, I was bare. 'Thank you. I like it, too.'

Eric didn't back up. He stayed close to my face, his breath on my cheek. His mouth nearly touching my ear. I

52

suppressed a shiver. 'Turn around for me so I can see. Up close.'

I turned slowly. I didn't even question why I was humouring him. He asked, I felt compelled to oblige. He still held my hand gently but firmly so I let my arm stretch out behind me as I turned. With my back to him, I waited. I held my breath. My skin felt as if it was on fire. When he touched me I heard a gasp tear out of me. A single fingertip. He traced the edges of the cut-out back, the gentlest touch I had ever felt and yet my head was swimming. He finally released my hand.

I stayed, frozen, back to him. Not moving. Unsure of what to do but determined not to break the spell that had settled over us. I heard the wine bottle bang on the table as he sat it down. His hands slid around my waist. He pulled me back so my ass was flush with a prominent erection. Another sound escaped me, this time a sigh. My dress whispered as he spread his hands across my waist and anchored me. He bent in low again, another kiss of hot breath against my throat. 'Would it scare you terribly if I asked you to come upstairs with me?'

I shook my head. My voice could not be trusted. Words would not come to me. I just shook my head. No. It would not scare me. Not at all.

I allowed myself to be led through the crowd. The smoke was thick, laughter loud, music blaring. No one noticed us. No one cared. Up the steps, I walked, hand back in his. My heart beating erratically and a pulse throughout my body. Captivated. Spell. I had no idea and I did not care. I wanted him. It was that simple.

My dress made secretive sounds against my stockings as I ascended. I did take a moment to thank the lingerie gods or whoever it was who put it in my head to wear the sexy unmentionables tonight. No standard pantyhose hiked up to my waist. No. My very best thong, the garter belt, the

53

seamed hose, the whole nine yards. I smiled in the fading light. I was very thankful to whoever had guided my hand.

The party noises faded as we made our way down the darkened hallway. My hand still nestled in his, I felt a slight moisture seep from me, staining the crotch of my panties with a wet warmth. I managed to draw a breath and fight off the light headed feeling.

'Won't Derek mind us being up here?' I whispered. 'I only know him from work. I'd hate–'

'I've known him since I was nine. He won't mind,' he whispered right against my lips and kissed me.

I sank into the kiss. Into him. Wantonly. Like I never had before. I pressed along the full length of him, feeling his body meld against mine. I opened my mouth, accepted his tongue and met it thrust for thrust. He tasted sweet. Like wine and candy. Like sinful things.

'In here.' He propelled me through a door, his mouth never leaving mine, the kiss never letting up.

I shoved my hands into his dark hair, grabbed handfuls as if I could kiss him more deeply if I held on for dear life. My back slammed against the wall and I used the resistance to arch my pelvis against him. Positioned myself to feel the delicious slide of his hard cock along the seam of my sex. I hummed my appreciation and continued the kiss. Let myself get lost in the slick humid moisture that was his mouth.

He broke away first and I found myself instinctively chasing after his mouth with my own, intent on reconnecting with him. He dropped to his knees and ran his hand up the inside of my calf and rested his forehead against my belly. 'What's on under this deceptive dress, Ash? It's been driving me insane since I saw you come through the front door. Proper pantyhose? Thigh highs with elastic, which is cheating by the way. Thong? Bikinis? Nothing? I've been dying to find out.'

His large hand moved up to my knee and just a touch beyond. I was panting in the dark. I could hear myself. There wasn't enough air and only a tiny bit of light. An antique table lamp that gave off no more light than a nightlight. His hand stilled there, so warm and big that I thought my skin might ignite. 'May I?' he whispered, lips pressed flush against my abdomen. His words vibrated up my body sparking a blissful shiver.

'You may.'

I whispered it. I barely heard myself. He heard me, though. His hands started a slow northward ascent. The room so quiet I could hear the sensuous sound of his hands moving up my thighs. The sound so amplified by silence and the adrenaline in my body, it sounded unbelievably loud. His hands reached the tops of my thighs. The sweet spot where the stockings were secured by the snaps of my garter. I hitched in a breath as he murmured appreciatively and dipped a finger below the gauzy material.

'This is what I was thinking,' he sighed and kissed the vee of my thighs through my dress. One chaste kiss and I was soaked. I felt it rush from me and my nipples hardened. 'I was hoping... praying, actually, that I would find something like this if I managed to get you alone. I saw the seams on the back of the stockings. I had to know,' he laughed quietly and the sound was like being stroked, 'if they were the real deal or a cheap imitation. I would have been very disappointed to find thigh highs with elastic. A woman like you should wear the classics.'

A woman like me. A woman who, at the moment, couldn't form a coherent sentence if her life depended on it.

Eric lifted my dress almost demurely. A slight tug of the fabric, a nearly dainty motion, like drawing up a curtain. Without thinking, I took the hem and gathered it to my waist. Holding it out of his way and offering myself up for display.

'And this thong… perfect,' he breathed and this time his breath feathered across my belly. I felt the fine hair stir and lift in its wake. I pulled the fabric tighter against myself just to do something, to take my mind from the fact that I felt unstable. Consumed. Just by his gaze.

First his eyes and then his fingers, warm and blunt, outlined the satin triangle of my thong. Heat blossomed in my cheeks and my chest, spreading like liquid fire down to my cunt. I made a small noise in my throat.

'Do you trust me?' he murmured, kissing the soft skin that bordered my panties. My entire body weight pressed against the wall. I nodded, though I had no reason to trust him. Not a reason in the world. But I did. Instinctively, I trusted him.

His lips never left my body but his voice got a little louder, 'I need you to tell me. Out loud. Do you trust me?'

'Yes,' I whispered.

As soon as my answer fell from my lips, he began. He released my stocking from their clips. The now empty straps brushed against my bare thighs. Eric peeled the stockings slowly, rolling one down with exaggerated care and patience. When he lifted my foot free, he put the rolled stocking carefully aside. The other leg received the same care. By the time both stockings were laid neatly on the floor, I was barely breathing. Taking in just enough oxygen to stay alive. His fingers hooked in the side straps of my thong and he tugged gently then stopped. He kissed the stripe of naked flesh above the waistband and then slowly dragged the scrap of material from me.

I could hear it whispering in the near dark. The fabric sounded almost as joyous and aroused as I felt. When the thong pooled around my ankles, he lifted first one foot then the other to set my legs free. Then he stood. Stockings in one hand, thong in the other.

'Now, Ash, I want you to turn around for me. Face the wall.'

The words startled me but the tone soothed. Demanding but gentle. Meant to be obeyed but also meant to set me at ease. He lowered his head, sucked my nipple into his mouth and sucked until a stripe of fire shot from my breast to my sex. 'Go on, now. Turn around.'

I did it without hesitation.

Eric's trailed his knuckles down the base of my spine, I could feel the satin and nylon he held rasping against my skin. I shivered when he leaned in, his breath hot on my neck. He bit me just hard enough to make me whimper and make my nipples pucker. The pleasure from the pain slid over my skin as I tried to figure out his plans. He bent down and I felt that hot breath on the base of my spine.

'Spread your legs for me,' he said calmly. I felt anything but calm. Scared, excited, bad. I felt all of those things but not calm. He pushed his palms against my bare calves, forcing my stance wider. I felt the slippery nylon loop around my ankle and then he moved to my left. The hosiery snickered in the near darkness as I watched him tie it to a dresser leg. 'Now the other,' he murmured as if he were talking to himself. My right ankle was encompassed and then he moved to tie it to the foot of the antique bed.

Eric stood and slid his hands along my sides, dragging my dress up with him. He lifted it over my head as I held my arms up like a child. 'The bra can stay,' he whispered and kissed me for a few moments. His tongue warm and sweet with wine. The gentleness of the kiss helped the fear beating away in my chest calm a little.

I stood with my legs bound wide, feeling like a prisoner ready for frisking. Instead of feeling embarrassed, I felt incredibly powerful. I could feel his eyes on me. Feel him studying me and soaking in the site of me splay legged and nearly naked just for him. 'Arms above your head, Ash.

57

Normally, I'd like to bind them behind your waist but you seem just a little nervous. It's not as scary if they're bound above your head.'

I almost told him to go for it. Tie them behind my back. I didn't. His judgment was probably better than mine in this situation. I was a virgin at being trussed up. He obviously, had done this before. I slid my hands up the plaster wall and clasped my hands together.

'Do you have any idea how spectacular your back looks like that? A work of art. Those long lean muscles taut and tense. You are a vision.' His voice snaked into my ear and my nipples grew harder, little pebbles pushing eagerly against the black lace of my bra.

He looped my own thong around my wrists, tying it tighter than I had expected. His tongue dragged the length of my neck from nape to base and then another bite was administered. The insides of my thighs felt hot and slick. My body pulsed. All I wanted was for him to fuck me. My world had narrowed down to the stranger standing behind me. To the nylon that circled my ankles and the satin that bound my hands. And my vulnerability. I was helpless and the thought of being helpless for him brought a flicker in my cunt that was damn near close to an orgasm. A little burst of hot pleasure that demanded more pleasure in turn.

I heard his zipper, the rustle of fabric. The almost inaudible sound of clothes being tossed to the floor. I waited.

He smoothed his hands over my back, his words ringing in my mind as he slid his warm palms over each muscle in my back. I shivered. Then his hands gripped my hips and yanked me back. I nearly lost my balance but Eric kept me steady. I balanced as best I could, legs set wide, ass thrust backwards, hands above my head. Beyond doing my best I had to trust him.

Two fingers dipped into me, sliding into my warm waiting body. I sighed.

'You are very ready, aren't you? Positively dripping. Do you want me to fuck you, Ash? I need you to answer. No nodding that pretty little head. I need you to say it.'

Though my face grew so hot I felt feverish, I took a deep breath and said it. 'I want you to fuck me, Eric. Please,' I added for good measure and without thinking I stuck my ass out further. Beckoning. Pleading with my body.

The growl rumbled from low in his chest, his hands bit into my hips and he shoved into me so fast my breath stuck in my throat. Then I sighed, sinking thankfully back onto his cock as he fucked me.

I wasn't much good on trust. Not under the best of circumstances. Nearly dark, tied up, with a stranger wouldn't be considered the best of circumstances. Many men had taught me that trusting a male of the species was an earmark of stupidity. For whatever reason, I trusted him, though. I trusted him to have me bound, keep me nearly blind, and fuck me. It was freeing, this blind trust and I let the thought slip from my mind as he pushed a little higher. The head of his cock was smacking my G spot repeatedly. I tried to fight the orgasm, the clench that was beyond my control as my body gripped his. I lost. A spectacular loss that was trumpeted with wave after wave of pressure and release. All I could do was rest my forehead against the cool plaster as I sobbed out my pleasure.

'Good, good, girl,' he whispered against my ear. His hands roamed the taut muscles of my ass as my cunt continued to flicker and jump around his cock. 'Don't move. Stay just as I have you.'

He pulled from my body and I felt empty. Cold. I wanted him back.

'Be patient,' he whispered as if he could read my thoughts. 'I'm not done with you. Not in any sense of the word.' He untied the stockings, readjusted them so that my legs were even farther apart. My body even more vulnerable. Once the knots were retied, he slid along the wall so that he was in front of me. My bound hands over his head, my breasts smashed to his chest. I realised I would give anything if he'd take off my bra and suck my nipples, but I didn't ask.

'Now, I want to see what you taste like after you come,' he said. He kissed me. A fleeting kiss than left me wanting more. And though he didn't remove my bra, he yanked the cups down and nibbled slowly on one nipple and then the other. By the time his tongue left a hot trail of spit over my belly button and towards my waiting pussy, I was light-headed.

His mouth found me. Lips and tongue and teeth doing a spectacular dance across my pussy lips, suckling my clit. The rigid tip of his tongue swooped into me and he murmured against me, most likely at the taste of my come. I tried to stay steady flattening my upper body against the wall and prayed I wouldn't fall over. His hands gripping my waist tightly were the only things that kept me from sinking to the floor. Of that I was certain.

Only when I came again, a second crushing orgasm that wet his face and lips, did he release me. When he came up and kissed me he tasted like wine and my moisture. I could have kissed him all night. Even as he kissed me, his fingers stayed busy, playing and kneading. Stroking my clit, sliding into my cunt, keeping me perpetually on the edge of another orgasm.

'Are you OK? Not uncomfortable?' he asked.

His teeth went back to work on my nipple and the sensation shot straight to my cunt. I moaned but managed a weak. 'No. fine.'

'Good.' Then he was gone. Behind me again. His presence fiercely palpable.

60

I felt his cock rub against my slit again as my body jumped eagerly. Back in me. That's what I wanted. Him back in me, moving, slamming, pounding. While I remained helpless and at his mercy. Just the thought made me push back against him, trying desperately to speed up his re-entry.

'Behave. Don't move.' I felt his erection break contact with my body. Punishment, I assumed. I breathed. One breath, two breaths, three breaths…

Without warning he slid into me. One forceful stroke that filled me completely and left me gasping. His hands covered my hands as he leaned his full weight against me, pressing me to the wall, smashing me. His cock slammed high and fast as he grunted in my ear and I kissed the cool plaster beneath my lips. Teeth bit down in the soft flesh of my shoulder and I came again. My keening wail complimented the guttural sound of him spilling into me. He jerked against me forcefully as our combined orgasm took over.

We rode out the silence and the aftershocks. His large fingers encircling my bound wrists. I could feel his heart beat slamming against my shoulder blade. The bite on my shoulder sang with the sweetest pain. Like being branded, marked. I felt owned. And oddly, safe.

'Don't move.' Eric untied my wrists and I felt pins and needles settle instantly in my flesh. I kept my hands together, arms raised, afraid to break the spell.

I heard him bend down. Heard the whispers of nylon as he untied my hose. Felt the slack in my thighs as the tension disappeared and the burn of my trembling muscles. I stayed in that position too. Legs spread wide. I wouldn't move until I was told I could.

'Turn around.'

I did. I faced him. He smiled. The most handsome smile I had ever seen. A secret smile just for me. I had been at his

61

mercy and now I felt oddly protected by him. I didn't question it, I just smiled back.

'I want you to leave this alone,' he said, helping me step back into my thong. 'Don't wipe me away. Leave it. Let my come dry. I want it in you, on you and on these lovely delicates. OK?'

I nodded as he slipped the sidebands onto my hips. I could feel it pooling in the cotton crotch. Hot and thick. In my head I could picture its milky opaque texture. I could smell it, too. The room was thick with the smell of pussy and come and sex. I smiled again.

He slid my stockings up my thighs and it felt beyond sensual. To be dressed, to be tended to. I was sore and happy and a little confused. He adjusted the clasps and murmured to himself, 'looks as if they only stretched a touch.' I didn't care.

Next came the dress. He slid it over my head, adjusted the seams, smoothed the wrinkles. He fluffed my hair and helped me back into my shoes. Then he held my head in his big strong hands and kissed me. The same kind of kiss that had started it all. I fell into it. Let myself go. Nothing mattered but his hot mouth, his velvety tongue and the feel of him cradling my head.

'Do you trust me?' he asked again.

'Yes.' This time I knew to say it out loud. I meant it. Now I had reason to trust him.

'Good. You're coming home with me.' It wasn't a question.

'Of course.'

Michael's Surprise
by Eva Hore

'So honey, do you want to give it a go?' Michael said, coming up behind me, nuzzling into my neck.

'I'm not sure,' I said. 'I don't like the idea of being tied up and blindfolded.'

'Come on, we've done it before.'

'Not blindfolded we haven't.'

'What's the difference. It'll make it more exciting. You won't know what I'll do next,' he said, giving me a wolfish look. 'You won't know what part I'll ravish next. Your breasts, pussy or that sexy arse of yours. You'll love it.'

'Stop it,' I said giggling, his hand sliding up my skirt.

'Well?' he pleaded boyishly.

'OK,' I said.

Michael could be so persuasive. He was a fantastic husband, always trying to please me, making sure I was satisfied before he came himself. He was constantly surprising me with new experiences. I loved it.

'Here, let me finish these off. You go and have a quick shower,' he said stacking the dishwasher.

I took up his offer. Entering the bedroom I gasped. He'd strewn rose petals all over the bed. Candles lit up the room and music was playing on the CD player. He'd thought of everything. What more could a woman ask for?

I let my soapy hands slowly wash over my breasts, in between the folds of my pussy, and down my legs. The water washed away the tension of the day, allowing me to relax with thoughts of what pleasures were to come.

Sitting on the chair in front of the mirror I looked critically at myself. I applied light make-up. Rubbed cream into my neck, legs and arms. I smiled to myself, wondering what tonight would hold.

I was so busy with my thoughts I didn't notice Michael had come into the room. He kissed the back of my neck inhaling his favourite perfume.

The blindfold came up and quickly covered my eyes.

'You look very sexy,' he said, taking me by the shoulders, helping me to stand.

I still had the towel wrapped around me. His fingers tugged at it in between my breasts. Very slowly he unwrapped me, holding the towel open before dropping it to the floor. I stood there naked, waiting.

'Michael,' I said, wondering where he was.

'Hmm,' he said, behind me.

'Oh,' I said, startled. 'I didn't know you were there.'

'That's the whole idea.'

His fingers gently glided over my body, causing goose bumps to appear all over my skin. I shivered in anticipation when his tongue licked the inside of my thighs.

I felt disorientated. I swooned backwards, my legs opening to him. He grabbed my cheeks firmly with his hands and buried his face into me, then abruptly he stopped and led me to the bed.

Lying down amongst the rose petals was intoxicating as the aroma wafted up, exciting my senses. Something fluttered over me and I realised he was sprinkling rose petals.

Michael sat astride me. He took both my hands in his and stretched them outwards. He lightly ran his fingers from the tips of mine, across and under my armpit and back again. I lay there, arms outstretched, feeling his balls lightly brush my skin as he leaned across to snap on the handcuffs.

It was an amazing feeling, lying there like that, seeing nothing, not knowing where he was and what he was going to do next. I felt exposed, nervous, paranoid. It was ridiculous.

Michael had seen every inch of me, but for some reason, it was as if we were doing this for the first time. I couldn't look into his eyes to see what they were saying. It might just as well have been a stranger, a new man who was still unknown territory.

His tongue circled my nipples, licking and nipping, then trailed between my legs to linger on the lips of my pussy. I moaned quietly, enjoying the sensation. Suddenly, his hands ran down the inside of my thighs to my ankles, roughly yanking my legs apart.

I gasped as he tied each ankle, then gave my thighs a quick smack.

'Hey,' I said, 'I didn't expect that.'

'Shh,' was all he said.

I was slightly annoyed, but then realised that this was the whole point of what we were doing. Expecting the unexpected. I relaxed when I felt his tongue again, licking me, opening the folds of my pussy.

His tongue probed deeper. His fingers sought out my breasts, tugging my nipples, making them erect. His hands ran down the outside of my body, his fingers firmly massaging as they went, until they reached my feet.

He moved off. I lay there breathing hard, excited, trying to anticipate what would come next. I sensed his return and was surprised when something was pushed in between my lips, making me open my mouth.

It was a strawberry, coated in delicious chocolate. Mmmm, lovely. The chocolate was just beginning to melt when Michael pulled it away. He rubbed my lips with it, crushing the fruit, smearing it over my mouth and chin.

Then tiny droplets were falling on my face, neck, stomach. His hand moved. Droplets trickled down the lips of my pussy. My mouth was open, waiting, tongue searching. A small piece of watermelon dropped inside. I sucked the juice and swallowed, savouring the taste.

A glass was put to my lips, and I smelt the unmistakable heady vapour of cognac, my favourite liqueur. I gulped, as it was poured into my mouth, burning the back of my throat, causing heat to radiate throughout my body when it hit the pit of my stomach.

Cognac was dribbled over my body. A hungry mouth licked my lips, nibbling at the strawberry, tasting the cognac mingled with the juices from the watermelon and then attacked my pussy with gusto.

I could feel myself coming and pushed my pussy up into his face, grinding my pelvis, wanting his cock inside me, to satisfy me fully, but he pulled back, leaving me there, frustrated and panting.

He brushed his cock against my mouth. I opened wide trying to grab it, to suck it into my mouth. He teased me with it, leaving it at my lips, only to quickly withdraw, once I had captured the head and slid down the shaft.

'Michael, please,' I mumbled. 'Fuck me, will you.'

He laughed and left me there, my pussy open, begging for attention.

There was a noise on the other side of the room. I gasped as lots of tiny fingers ran over my body. I knew it had to be a whip. I smiled to myself, enjoying this exciting experience.

My smile was short lived as I felt the sting of those fingers flick like lightening, burning my thigh.

'Hey, that hurt.'

'You love it,' he said, whipping me again. 'I can see how wet you're getting.'

Gently now, the whip covered my left foot. Slowly and sensually it travelled up the inside of my thigh, caressing and tickling me as it went. He reached my pussy and I felt the handle probing about. I arched upwards. If I couldn't have his cock, I guess the whip would at least satisfy me temporarily.

He wasn't giving it me that easily. I struggled at the restraints and opened my mouth to protest. The blindfold had shifted and let in a sliver of light.

I wanted to see his face, to see his reaction to my part of this game. I needed to see if he was enjoying this as much as I was.

But it wasn't Michael! Steven, his best friend, was standing there between my legs flicking the whip. My first thought was yelling at him to stop. My second was that I was enjoying this game. I wondered where Michael was.

My mouth turned into a silent 'O', when I saw Michael sitting on the chair in front of my dressing table, with Vanessa, Steven's wife, straddling him. She was riding his cock like there was no tomorrow and Michael was watching her arse in the mirror as he pulled her cheeks apart.

The bastard!

Vanessa had approached me a few weeks ago regarding wife swapping and I'd told her we we'd let her know. I was keen on the idea but Michael said he needed time to think about it. Now I knew he must have already set this up as a surprise for me.

I felt myself throb madly as I watched the two of them. I wondered why I hadn't noticed that they'd joined in. Having discarded the whip, Steven was now licking me to distraction. A rush of juices escaped me as I anticipated what it would be like, him fucking me.

I thrashed around moaning.

'Oh, God, yeah,' I said. 'That's fucking fabulous.'

I wanted my hands around his head, so I could pull him in closer, hold him there. My legs were begging to be wrapped around him like a vice so I could mesh him into me.

His mouth was setting me on fire. My vision was blurred from passion. I peered over to where Michael was. They'd moved from the chair. He now had her bent over, doggy style, at the edge of the bed, so they could all see the action. Her breasts were swaying backwards and forwards with each thrust.

'Oh, God. Fuck me, will you. Fuck me hard, you bastard,' I screamed.

It was time I joined this party.

Michael was watching Steven, and wondered what he was thinking. Vanessa was now on her knees, sucking Michael's cock Her eyes followed Steven as he rose up on the bed.

I could hardly stand the wait. He had a fabulous cock, the skin so stretched and shiny that the veins looked about ready to burst. I watched fascinated as he fell to his knees before me, his arms bracing himself on either side of me, obviously not wanting me to know it wasn't Michael's body.

'For fuck's sake, hurry up,' I screamed.

I felt the tip of his cock enter me.

'Oh, fuck, Michael. Your cock is so fucking great. Give it to me.'

With that he plunged straight in. I was so wet he slipped in and out easily, the juices running down onto his balls. The sensation was amazing. I could feel myself getting wetter with each stroke.

'Undo my legs, baby,' I begged, 'so I can wrap them around you. Will you fucking well hurry?' I demanded.

He quickly untied my legs and instantly I had them around him, humping into him, grinding my pelvis back and slamming into him with each new stroke.

This spurred Steven on even more and he started pumping furiously, holding me up by the hips off the bed, his fingers stretching beneath me to graze my hole. It was like I was splitting in two.

My breasts were flopping around all over the place, my arms stretched, my wrists aching as they rubbed against the handcuffs. The pain actually turned me on more, and I totally lost control, screaming for more, as the most powerful orgasm I've ever had burst through me.

Michael had Vanessa on the edge of the bed and I saw her grappling to hold onto something as he pumped her as hard as Steven pumped me. I felt Steven explode and was amazed that neither he nor Vanessa had uttered a single word.

For a moment I wondered if they were ever going to tell me, or if this was going to become a regular thing, with me supposedly being totally unaware.

Michael manoeuvred Vanessa directly in front of my pussy and as he pumped into her she lapped at me like a cat licking cream, my cream. I could stand it no longer.

'For God's sake, Michael,' I screamed. 'Get these handcuffs off me so I can really join in this party.'

'You know?' he asked, shocked.

'Of course I know. No-one's got a cock like yours, baby. Now get these cuffs off me so we can fuck our brains out.'

And we did!

70

Office Shenanigans
by Chloe Devlin

Margaret looked up from the brightness of her computer screen into the darkness of the suite of offices. Was that a noise she'd heard? A door closing perhaps? It couldn't be since she was alone here and she'd locked herself in. 'Who's there?'

Silence echoed back at her.

'I know I heard something,' she said. 'Tell me who's there.'

Dismissing the sound, she told herself that it was her imagination. She rapidly continued her typing, concentrating on the report, making sure she got each fact and figure correct. Mr Stinson was a stickler for details and wouldn't hesitate to fire her anyway if she got something wrong.

Sometimes she wanted to quit, she hated working there so much. Well, mostly she hated her boss. He was a real uptight asshole who never so much as cracked a smile. That wouldn't be that bad, except he was the most gorgeous, sexiest man she'd ever seen. Sometimes she got hot imagining that instead of leaning over her pointing out her mistakes, he was leaning over her to kiss her or touch her breasts.

She reached out to double-check her place on the page and caught a sudden movement out of the corner of her eye. Before she could swing around, a gloved hand clamped itself over her mouth and something cold and sharp pressed against her neck. She drew in a gasping breath, ready to scream.

'Don't move or make a sound,' a low voice hissed in her ear. 'I would hate to have to hurt you. I've been watching you,' the intruder said. 'Watching and wondering. All sorts of things. I wondered if your tits were real. If you were a natural redhead. I wondered if you liked to suck cock and if your pussy was hot and juicy.'

Her throat tightened. Who was this man?

A tongue swirled in her ear, sending shivers through her body, despite herself. 'And tonight I'm going to find out.'

Oh, Jesus, she thought. This guy was going to make her blow him, and then he was going to fuck her. She started to squirm, wondering if she could free herself enough to escape.

'Now here are the ground rules,' her rapist said. 'You don't scream or yell. One peep out of you and I gag you with your panties. I'm going to blindfold you. No peeking through or underneath. Your hands will be tied behind you, but I'll leave your legs free. If you don't open your legs when I say so or try to run or kick me, I'll tie you spread so wide you'll feel like a wishbone. Got it?'

She nodded.

'Now, take your hands off the keyboard, lean forward and put them behind you.'

Margaret followed the instructions, moving slowly so that the knife at her throat wouldn't cut her. When she had leaned far enough over the keyboard, her captor took his hand off her mouth. 'Remember. No noise. Now place the backs of your hands against each other.'

She struggled to obey him, then felt a pair of cold handcuffs slide over her wrists and snap shut. Once she was cuffed, the knife was removed from her throat and he slipped a black elastic blindfold over her eyes, blocking out the meagre light from her desk lamp.

'Much better,' he said. 'Now it's time for some fun.' He spun her chair around. 'Stand up.'

Her tied hands threw her off balance. Finally, she stood there, tottering on her heels, her chest thrust out because of her cuffed wrists. She listened intently, trying to figure out where he was by the sound of his breathing.

He guided her several steps to the side and then backwards. She stopped when she felt the rough edge of a desk against the backs of her legs. His hands came up under her arms. 'Hop up,' he said and hoisted her up to sit on the desk.

Pushing her down on her back so that her head hung over the far end, he trailed one hand over her body as he walked around the desk. She heard the rasp of a zipper, followed by the scuffling noises of clothes being removed.

One finger on either side of her mouth pried it open, tipping her head back even farther. Before she could protest, he filled her mouth with his cock, stuffing it past her lips and down her throat.

She swallowed convulsively several times, trying not to gag. The tightness must've acted as a stimulant because his dick immediately stiffened. The longer and harder it grew, the easier it slid down her throat. Her captor held her head still while he pumped his hips.

'Aah, that feels good,' he groaned. 'I knew you'd have a hot mouth, my sweet. Just open wide and let me fuck my cock down your throat.'

She'd never had a guy talk to her like this. Despite the circumstances, she liked it. It made her feel sexy and hot. Maybe she was really a slut at heart, loving to suck and get

73

fucked. The thought that she was going to get fucked after this made her hot. Funny how a situation could completely turn around. She might have been tied up, blindfolded and stripped at knifepoint, but she couldn't deny that this forced cocksucking was making her hot. She could feel her nipples hardening against her bra and her crotch was already wet with anticipation.

She swirled her tongue around the huge cock that was invading her throat, sucking hard on the shaft, instead of passively letting it penetrate her. Another groan from her captor told her that he liked what she was doing and she began to avidly lick and suck at him.

His thrusts got harder and faster, going deeper down into her throat. 'That's right, my sweet,' he said. 'That's good. Keep sucking! Harder! Faster! Oh, God, I'm going to come.'

As he began to squirt into her mouth, he grasped her head and held it still, shoving the entire length of his huge cock down her throat, holding it there as his belly convulsed against her. Automatically she swallowed to keep from drowning, tasting the sweetness that slid down the back of her throat into her stomach.

After her tightly suctioned lips pulled the last drops out of his prick, he slowly drew it out of her mouth, wiping the tip around her cheeks. She stuck out her tongue, trying to get the last drops.

'I needed that,' he said. 'Keeping an eye on you has kept me worked up for days. But that took the edge off.'

She was afraid to ask him what his plans were. What if they weren't as sexy or kinky as she was hoping? Would she be disappointed? My God, what a slut she was. She had just been forced to suck a guy off while still totally clothed and all she could hope was that the rest of the night was as sexy and kinky as this had been.

74

His hands came up behind her head, lifting her into an upright position, seated on the desk. Then he moved around to stand in front of her and push her legs apart. She sat there, biting her lip, knowing that if he touched her crotch he would find it drenched. She jumped as she felt one finger swipe up from bottom to top of her panty-covered slit.

'Wet,' he said. 'Absolutely soaking wet. Well, that just makes things easier. I won't have to worry about tearing you. Hop down off the desk,' he ordered, then steadied her as she obeyed his command, tottering in her heels.

She felt fingers at the top of her blouse. He quickly stripped her blouse and skirt off, leaving her in her bra and panties. The cold edge of the knife slid up one hip, under the material of her panties. When he gave a yank, it easily slit the silk. He repeated this on her other hip, then pulled the two halves of her panties away from her body.

Afraid to say a word, she held herself perfectly still as the knife traced a pattern from the top of her pubic hair up and over her stomach until the sharp edge ripped open her bra. He cut every possible strap so the garment hung in tatters from her shoulders before he pulled it away from her, leaving her with nothing but a blindfold on.

'Don't worry. I'm not going to hurt your pretty body,' he said. 'Unless you disobey me and I have to.' She heard him set the knife down. Then he trailed a finger over her shoulder and collar bone and down to the swell of her tit. His fingertip felt rough on her soft skin, but somehow sensuous and her nipples tightened into painfully hard buds. She no longer wondered how that could be. It was obvious she was turned on.

Maybe it was that she didn't truly feel in any physical danger yet. Yes, she was handcuffed and blindfolded. And though he had just fucked her mouth and then stripped her, so far he had caused her no pain.

His wandering finger flicked her nipple, though. 'Look at this,' he murmured. 'Are you cold or just glad to see me?' He flicked the other nipple, causing a ripple of sensation to run through her body.

'Please,' she whispered.

'Please what, my sweet?'

'Please,' she repeated, shaking her head. She wasn't quite sure what she was pleading for.

'Perhaps you want me to do this.' His fingers pinched her bud between them, sending shooting sensations from her breasts to her groin. 'Or even this.' He pulled her breasts away from her body, using just her nipples, stretching them to an unbearable length.

She shivered from the feelings, wondering how much more she could take. A lot more, she thought, excitedly hoping that he would continue with this sexy torture.

'Spread your legs,' he commanded.

She immediately shifted her feet apart.

'Wider.'

She inched her heels away until she felt like she would fall if she moved anymore. What was she thinking? She was tied up against her will and being forced to perform sex acts on a total stranger. So why was she so hot and bothered? Unwilling to analyse the situation any longer, she let herself go with the flow, enjoying the sex acts as though this man was her steady boyfriend, a position that was currently vacant.

Her captor chuckled. 'Are you beginning to enjoy my touch? Let's try this!'

This turned out to be a large finger thrust up into her dripping pussy. She shoved her entire body at him, silently willing him to make her come. She knew it wouldn't take much. Just a few more thrusts of his finger and she'd climax heavily. But before that could happen, he removed his finger. She had to stifle her small whimper of dismay that this wondrous sensation had been withdrawn.

'Not yet, my sweet. I have other plans for you.' Her captor's voice was hoarse with longing as he guided her back to the desk. He lifted her onto the smooth wood top and laid her back.

As he positioned her so that she was at the edge of the desk, her head tilted backwards off the other side. But this time, he didn't come around to have her suck him off. Instead, he remained between her spread thighs. She could feel the heat from his body as he leaned up against her dripping cunt.

'It's time for some more fun,' he said. 'I wonder which part of this you'll enjoy better. Clips on your tits or my tongue on your clit.'

She held perfectly still, lying awkwardly with her still cuffed hands underneath the small of her back. The thought of him licking her pussy sent a fresh wave of desire through her. She only hoped that he would let her come, at least once.

A drawer rattled open next to her right thigh. He rummaged around, placed something on the desk, then slammed the drawer shut.

When she felt his hands on her breasts, she held her breath, unsure of the pain to come. But instead, he used his fingers to massage her tit, plumping it between his palms, pinching the tender nipple to hardness.

'What a lovely tit,' he crooned as he worked. 'So nice and round, not fake at all. And your nipples are a sight to see. Long and big and stiff as little acorns right now. Just the perfect thing for a small binder clip to clamp onto. Now, take a deep breath and hold it.'

As she did, he released the clip onto her right nipple. Her breath rushed from her lungs in response to the sharp sting of pain that filled her chest. She hissed in response, trying desperately not to cry out.

'Again,' he ordered. Without thinking, she obeyed, holding her breath until he attached the clip to her other nipple. She clenched her teeth to keep from screaming at the pain that doubled through her.

Her captor leaned over her, his chest pressing against her tortured tits, pressing the clips even harder into her breasts. 'When I kiss you, you have my permission to scream,' he said. 'But only when I kiss you.'

He pressed his open mouth against hers, his tongue sliding deep inside. She cried out several times, the sounds completely muffled by his kiss. Finally, she stopped shrieking and started kissing him back. He let her do this for several seconds before drawing away.

'You're doing very well, my sweet,' he complimented her. 'Now for the second half of this part.'

He lifted his body from hers, letting her lay there, the cool air rushing over her bare body. She heard the sound of rollers on the floor as he moved a chair between her legs. Then his hands clamped on her inner thighs, holding her still.

She held her breath again, willing him to lick her throbbing pussy. His hot breath washed over her quivering cunt. A sigh escaped her as the thin point of his tongue touched her dripping lips, then slid inside her pussy. He withdrew, then slowly traced a design up and down her labia.

She whimpered when he drew back. 'Please,' she whispered.

'We've been through this before. Please what, my sweet?'

She hesitated, her nipples throbbing in their torture, her pussy dripping with her juices. 'Please... please lick me,' she forced the words out.

'Lick what?'

'My… my pussy,' she stuttered. 'Oh, God, I need you to lick me. Make me come.'

'Your wish is my command.'

As though her words had released his restraint, he leaned forward, devouring her flesh. His tongue scoured every inch of her aching pussy, seeking out every nerve ending and torturing it with pleasure.

The waves shot through her body, zinging off her stinging nipples back to her swollen cunt. He ran the tip of his tongue around her sex lips several times before plunging it deep inside her repeatedly, fucking her with his tongue. He slid his tongue out of her and traced a pattern lower, circling her asshole. She clenched her anus in shock and surprise, then released the muscle, enjoying his probing tongue in that orifice.

After he thoroughly wetted her behind, he returned to her pussy, sucking the juices out of her. When she began to pant in ecstasy, he left her cunt and concentrated on her clit, alternately licking at the sensitive bud, then applying hard suction all around it.

She had never imagined these sensations before. They were unlike anything she'd ever experienced during sex. And it was even more incredible because of the situation. Instead of being in a nice bed with a considerate lover, she was blindfolded, cuffed and clamped on top of a desk being ravished by an unknown captor.

Exquisite pleasure shot through her quivering body and she squirmed against the rising tide, but her captor stayed with every thrust she made until her body went rigid under the onslaught. He gripped her spread thighs even tighter and nipped at her exposed, bulging clit. Margaret gave a shriek at the unexpected sensation, immediately stifling the noise by biting her lip. Her back arched involuntarily even further until she was almost bowed.

'Oh, God,' she moaned. 'I'm coming. I can't help it. I'm coming!'

Finally, after what seemed like hours of the beautiful pleasure, her captor released her clit and she slumped back down on the desk, her wrists still cuffed behind her back, her nipples still throbbing in their binder clips. An unbelievable feeling of satiated lust fell over her as she took in deep breaths, trying to calm her pounding heart.

'Delicious, my sweet,' her captor said. 'You are marvellous. Here, taste.'

He pulled her into a sitting position on the edge of the desk, then kissed her. His mouth was warm and wet and tasted of her own juices. Instead of being repulsed, she found it a turn-on and wondered if he could taste the faint residue of his semen on her tongue.

'I think it's time to take the blindfold and the cuffs off,' her attacker said. 'I believe I can trust you not to run or scream.'

Who was this man, Margaret wondered? Obviously he had no fear that she was going to report this to the police. But why would she? She'd never felt so much pleasure in her life. If her captor was someone she knew, she wanted to convince him to keep her.

'But I'll leave the binder clips on,' he continued. 'I think they'll add to what's to come.'

She heard a small click as he unlocked the metal handcuffs. She brought her hands around her front, massaging the aches in her wrists and arms from being bound like that. Then her captor reached around her head and untied the knot back there. Slowly he lifted the blindfold away from her eyes and took a step backwards.

She blinked against the sudden brightness. Even though there was only one light on, it seemed like a thousand floodlights. She glanced down, suddenly more aware of her kinky nakedness than ever before. She almost wished he'd put the blindfold back on. She'd felt much freer behind the anonymity of it.

Then she raised her eyes a fraction of an inch and saw a pair of legs standing in front of her. She forgot about the aches and pains in her wrists and arms. Ever so slowly, she raised her gaze inch by inch, taking in the beauty of the masculine form in front of her.

Strong thighs topped long muscular legs. His hips were slim, but beautifully framed his cock and balls. She stopped there for a moment and swallowed hard. His cock stood at attention, inches from his washboard flat belly, its bulbous head capping off an impressive shaft that had to be at least nine or ten inches long.

She continued her perusal up his flat stomach, over his well-defined pecs and chest until she reached his face. Her breath caught in her throat, stifling her gasp of surprise.

Somehow she'd expected to know her captor, but she hadn't expected it to be her boss, J. Robert Stinson. 'But… you…'

He laid a finger on her lips. 'I've wanted you for a long time. Wanted to do this with you. Tonight seemed like the perfect opportunity. I'd give you the option to leave if you were uncomfortable. But you're so wet, I know you're enjoying this. You can't deny it.'

She didn't want to. Somehow this man had tapped into her secret fantasies, making them come true. She wasn't about to walk away from that. 'Now what?'

'Now what, *sir*,' he said. 'You will call me sir, both in private and public.'

'Now what, sir?'

'Would you like to be fucked?'

In response, her nipples throbbed in their captivity. 'Oh, yes, sir,' she answered. 'Please fuck me!'

He stared at her spread thighs and clamped nipples a moment longer, then snapped his fingers. 'Off the desk and follow me.'

Margaret awkwardly slid off the edge onto her heels, wobbling a bit, but keeping her balance. She followed her boss out of the common area of cubicles into his private office, watching his firm buttocks flex with every step. She'd always thought he was sexy, but had never dreamed he had such a toned body.

As she stepped inside, she automatically closed the door behind her. She was pretty sure there was no one else in the building after everything that had happened to her, but she wasn't taking any chances.

Her boss sprawled in his executive chair behind his large ornate wood desk. His thighs slouched open, letting his balls rest on the leather of the chair. 'Now I want you to ride me,' he said.

Gingerly, still feeling the effects from her orgasm and the continuous pleasure/pain of the binder clips, she straddled him, lowering herself until his hard shaft slid right up inside her. They both gave a sigh as her pussy enclosed his cock in its warmth and tightness.

Instinctively, she kept her feet on the floor and used her thigh muscles to raise and lower her body like a ballerina doing a plie, her hands resting on his shoulders to maintain her balance. Her boss leaned back in his chair, allowing her to do all the work as they pushed towards climax.

Bend after bend, she rose and fell on his shaft, feeling the hardness push into her body, then retreat, only to shove in again. Suddenly his hands gripped her waist, holding her still while his hips thrust up and down, pistoning his cock in and out of her captive pussy.

She froze, remaining still while he fucked her, then gasped and flew into an exquisite orgasm as leaned forward and flicked the binder clips on her nipples with his tongue.

Her inner muscles clamped down as hard as they could on his cock and she shivered all over.

He gave a shout, then held perfectly still as he came within her, his cock pulsing inside her throbbing body. She felt the warm rush of his semen as it shot up into her. After several shots, he lowered his hips and her body until she slumped against him in the chair, both of them breathing heavily, his large cock still buried in her clenching pussy. Simultaneously, they tried to draw air into their tortured lungs, to bring their heartbeats down.

The minutes ticked away, the silence broken only by their gasping breath. His arms held her so tightly against him that she could feel his heart pounding beneath her. 'Did you like that?'

'Do you need to ask?' she replied a little shyly. 'If you want to know that truth, I think I've been dreaming about you for a long time.'

'And I've been fantasizing about you also,' he replied, his hands gently caressing her sweaty back, combing through her tangled hair.

'I think it's time to go home, my sweet,' her boss said. 'I have just one question for you.'

A question for her? What on earth could he want to ask her? He was the one in charge, her master. 'Yes, sir?'

'Are you coming home with me, to be my companion, my sweet sex slave? Or shall we forget this night ever happened?' As he spoke, she felt his cock flex inside her. Even after their tremendous orgasm, he was still hard within her.

She caught her breath. She hadn't dared to think about the future, past this night. But now, he was offering her a dream come true. A dream she hadn't known she wanted until tonight. Margaret swallowed. 'I want to come home with you, sir. I want to belong to you, to be your sex slave.'

'Good.' His voice rumbled next to her ear. 'Then let's get out of here. I still have a load of come that's destined for your ass.'

Margaret sighed happily as he withdrew his still hard cock, leaving behind a tingling sensation that left her wanting more. And she knew she was going to get it. She couldn't wait. She was so glad that she had decided to work late tonight. She had a feeling she would be doing so more often now, especially with her sexy boss.

Punishing The Professor
by J. Carron

Harriet stood at the front door of the museum, arms folded tight against her chest. She checked her wristwatch for the umpteenth time and scowled.

The minutes ticked by slowly. The tiny courtyard was empty. A light breeze rustled through fallen leaves, sending them scurrying for cover beneath the ornate stone cloisters. The daylight was fading and it was getting colder.

'Where the hell is he?' she muttered, a piercing shiver running the length of her body.

She should be well on her way home by now, heading back to her cosy apartment. There was a bottle of wine in the fridge and a flick on TV she wanted to watch. But here she was, still at the museum long after the last visitors of the day had taken their leave.

She heard footsteps on the cobbles beyond the courtyard. But it was a false alarm, a tourist had taken a wrong turning. He spotted the 'closed' sign, turned on his heels and retreated into the gloom. Harriet prised her stiff arms apart, rubbed her hands together and blew hard on the pale white flesh.

Silently she cursed the curator. He was the one who had left her here to greet the out-of-hours visitor. Of course, he was very sorry to land it on her at the last minute, but he had plans, an engagement he just couldn't cancel at such sort notice. She had plans too, not that he paid any attention.

She cursed the visitor too, even though she knew very little about him. The curator said he was an academic, making a flying visit to view an exhibit or two as part of a research project. She closed her eyes and dipped her head. The prospect of spending her evening – yes, her evening – baby-sitting a stuffy scholar in a draughty museum sapped the last vestiges of strength from her aching bones. Why could he not visit during opening hours, like everyone else?

Harriet glanced at her watch again. She decided she would give him another minute. Then she was off. She would deal with the curator and any repercussions tomorrow, when she was slightly warmer, and a lot less pissed off. For now, the academic and his precious study could swing.

Retreating back into the building, Harriet gathered her coat, hat and gloves and set the security alarm. She left the building, pulling the heavy front door closed behind her. But just before the latch was due to click into place, she heard footsteps behind her. She turned to see her visitor jogging across the courtyard.

Harriet cursed again, the expletive muffled by the high lapels of her jacket.

'Sorry I'm late,' the man puffed, stopping to catch his breath. 'My flight was delayed.'

If only I'd been a minute or two quicker off the mark, she thought, releasing her grasp on the door handle. She tried to muster a welcoming smile, but the effort was too much.

'Come in,' she muttered, reluctantly pushing the door open again.

Harriet disabled the intruder alarm and slapped the lights on. As the neon strips flickered into life, she noticed the man was younger than she had expected. He didn't look like a stuffy professor. In fact, he was quite presentable. He wore denim jeans, a black roll-neck jersey and a black leather jacket. He dumped a scruffy leather satchel and overnight bag on the reception desk and extended a hand.

'My name's Robert Hale,' he smiled. 'I hope I haven't put you to too much trouble.'

'Harriet,' she replied, still scowling, her expression evidence, if it were needed, he had.

'My curator said there are a couple of exhibits you want to see,' she said frostily, ever mindful he was eroding her free time.

'Yes,' he replied. 'But first I need to make myself comfortable. I haven't stopped since I left the airport.'

She sighed. 'The toilets are along the corridor.'

He sauntered off and Harriet stood, tapping her fingers in frustration on the reception desk, edgily awaiting his return. Five minutes later he was back, smiling cheerfully.

'That's better.'

'Can we get on now?'

Either he failed to spot the abrupt tone, or chose to ignore it. He retrieved his satchel, opened it and slowly sifted through the contents. Harriet felt her irritation mount as the minutes ticked by. Eventually he pulled out a notebook and some photocopies. He handed one to her.

'I'd like to start with this one.'

She recognised the exhibit immediately.

'Follow me.'

She led him from the foyer into the main room of the museum, walking briskly, her heels clacking impatiently across the wooden floor. Robert Hale lagged behind. This angered her even more, but she bit her tongue. He loitered, his intent gaze surveying the pictures gracing the black walls. Most were crude line drawings. They depicted scenes of slaughter, of human suffering, of agony and torment.

Swords and axes, wielded aloft by grinning, manic-eyed men, lopped off heads and limbs at will. Men were hung, drawn and quartered. Women were burned at the stake, or drowned in ponds. And every picture showed great grinning crowds gathered to witness the medieval mayhem.

The museum also housed the physical evidence, the historical contraptions of execution and torture employed down the ages by the ruthless, the bloodthirsty and the plain sadistic.

'What do you think of our little collection, Mr Hale?' Harriet asked in an attempt to hurry him along.

'Professor Hale,' he pointed out.

'Professor Hale,' she repeated grudgingly.

'Remarkable, even if some of the interpretative material is a little questionable.'

Harriet stopped in her tracks. 'Questionable?'

'A little ghoulish, one might say.'

'One might, but it appeals to our visitors.'

Harriet knew that most of the people who visited the Museum of Torture were drawn through the doors by a primitive urge to see blood and gore. They were the type who slowed to view the aftermath of a road accident or motorway pile-up. The exhibits were designed to shock. No apology was made for that. But there was an historical context too, an important role in the creation of civilised society.

Rarely did academia grace the place with its hallowed presence. Harriet guessed this was why the curator was so keen to accommodate Professor Robert Hale. Perhaps the old fool thought it would lend some gravitas to his tacky tourist haunt. As far as she was concerned, if Professor Robert Hale didn't like the 'questionable' captions, he could fuck off.

She slapped her hand unrepentantly on hard wood.

'Here it is, the exhibit you were so keen to see – the rack.'

The professor approached the gruesome implement with a mixture of excitement and trepidation. He began furiously scribbling notes on his little pad, pausing occasionally to run his fingers over the polished oak, the worn leather cuffs, the rollers, the handles and the cogs.

'It's a very fine piece,' he whispered. 'Used during the Spanish Inquisition.'

She nodded. The 'questionable' caption said as much.

'Is that you finished then?' she asked hopefully.

'I've only just begun.'

Her heart slumped. She was in for a long and tortuous night herself.

Several long minutes dragged by before the professor spoke again. 'I have a small favour to ask,' he said. 'Will you put me on the rack?'

'Sorry?' Harriet was confused. She wasn't sure she heard him right.

'As part of my research I want to get a feel of what it was like for the unfortunate souls who were forced to undergo such horrific torture,' he explained.

'Well…' she hesitated. 'I'm not sure if that is… er… really possible.'

'You would be assisting me in my research,' he pointed out.

Reluctantly Harriet agreed. She remembered the curator's instruction – afford him every courtesy. With any luck he'd hop up, hop down and hop off out of the place. But as soon as she uttered the word 'OK', the professor darted out of the room, slightly flustered, telling her he'd be back in one minute.

In his absence, she set the rack up, unbuckling the wrist and ankle cuffs in preparation. It wasn't the first time she'd racked someone up: she often did it for the tourists. It was all part of the interactive museum experience. What she wasn't prepared for, however, was the professor's return. He re-entered the room wearing what appeared to be an old-fashioned nightgown. Tied loosely below the neck, the cotton garment hung to his knees. He spotted the look of bewilderment on Harriet's face straight away.

'It's for authenticity.'

She was barely able to stifle a snigger. He was, she grudgingly admitted to herself, a handsome and well-built man. But frankly he looked ridiculous in this absurd get-up.

Mindful of the time, Harriet gestured towards the rack and the professor climbed on, lying face down.

'You should be the other way up,' Harriet pointed out.

'A common misconception,' he replied. 'Many victims of this cruel device lay face down.'

Harriet awaited further explanation, but it was not forthcoming. She buckled the cuffs tightly around his wrists and ankles. She pulled one of the wrist straps rather too forcefully, causing the professor to exhale sharply. It gave her a little feeling of satisfaction. That'll teach you to keep me hanging around all night, she thought.

'I'm ready to be stretched,' he said. 'But not too far; I don't want any dislocated limbs.'

'Is that not the whole point?' Harriet mouthed the words silently to herself as she gripped the great wooden handle that turned the rollers. Slowly she rotated it. It was easy at first, but more pressure was needed as the professor's joints began to elongate and then finally stretch, the muscles tightening.

'Ooh!' he exclaimed.

She stopped. 'Is that enough?'

'Keep going.'

Harriet did. It was a rather liberating feeling, knowing she could, if she wanted to, inflict real pain upon the pompous professor. She recalled the moment he curtly corrected her when she addressed him as 'Mr Hale' and gave the handle a sharp twist.

Hale yelped. Harriet stepped back and noticed his arms and legs were at full stretch. The muscles in his shoulders and calves were as taut as the strings on a Stradivarius and the nightshirt was riding up his back. He wasn't wearing any underpants and the pale flesh of his white buttocks was starting to show. Harriet quickly averted her curious gaze.

'Are you OK?' she asked, worried she may have gone too far.

'Fine,' he whispered breathlessly.

'I'll roll it back.'

'No,' he protested.

'Victims often had pain inflicted upon them while they were on the rack. I want to feel that too,' the professor said.

'What do you want me to do?'

'A riding crop, a stick, something like that,' he suggested.

'You want me to hit you?'

His head nodded between rigid shoulders. Harriet hurriedly scoured the museum for suitable implements. *Afford him every courtesy.* She repeated the words in her head as she laid hands on a wooden paddle and a whip, the sort of things every good torture museum has lying around.

Harriet eyed them cautiously; she wasn't sure which to use first. She opted for the paddle. It was about the size of a table tennis bat, but without the blessing of rubber padding. She patted the rigid wood against Hale's buttocks.

'Harder,' he said.

She tightened her grip on the shaft and, with a flick of her wrist, brought it down sharply. The professor's body tensed and he let out a dull groan. Harriet wavered.

'Again,' he muttered insistently.

Smack, smack, smack, the slap of wood against flesh echoed through the empty hall.

Harriet smiled. God that felt good. She was enjoying herself. The tension and frustration of the evening was ebbing from her uptight body with every sadistic stroke. The nuisance of being kept waiting, the irritation of those five long minutes in the washroom, her annoyance at his condescending attitude towards the tags on the exhibits. And it was all in the name of academic research.

Smack, smack, smack, alternating between buttocks, the flesh reddening as she flicked the paddle up and down. The professor beseeched her to continue. He had really asked for it now and there was nothing he could do to stop her, his hands and feet were bound. The heady feeling of power was intoxicating. She realised she had complete control over him, this learned man, this educated man of words and books, lying helpless before her.

Harriet dropped the paddle and took up the whip.

'Why have you stopped?' the professor asked, unable to see her actions.

He had dictated to her long enough.

'I'm in charge now,' she said, running the tails through her fingers, preparing herself for the first lash. She was immersing herself in the role of captor. She would decide when it came, not him. That was the pleasure for her. He was the one on the rack and she was the one dishing out the punishment.

The professor remained completely still, bracing himself for the unknown. Harriet raised the whip above her head. She held it there for a lingering moment, watched his cheeks clench in anticipation. Then she brought it down, tails whipping across the bare flesh. Hale's body recoiled.

'Do you want me to do it again?' she asked.

'Yes.'

Harriet flicked the whip up and down, up and down. Hale's buttocks rolled in torment until at last he pleaded: 'Stop!' His bottom was glowing a rosy shade of rouge.

She laid the whip down and relaxed. Her breathing was fast and shallow. She felt her heart pound like a caged beast trapped beneath her ribcage. She rolled back the rack and released the professor's hands and feet. He eased himself up and sat uncomfortably. To her astonishment, she spotted an obvious protuberance below his nightshirt. He had an erection.

Harriet was uncertain how to respond. This was supposed to be academic research. He knew she had seen it. It was impossible to miss. He looked a little embarrassed. Moral indignation must surely be in order. But she was aroused too, there was no denying the satisfying warmth now radiating between her legs.

'There's another exhibit you should see,' Harriet prompted, no longer quite so eager to see him off the premises.

They crossed the floor together, Hale trying unsuccessfully to conceal the bulge of his groin. He was limping slightly after his time on the rack. She introduced him to a set of stocks.

'This ought to perk you up a bit,' Harriet said, no pun intended.

She stepped up to the instrument of restraint. 'If you don't mind, I'd like to give this one a go.'

'By all means,' he conceded.

She lowered her neck on to the smooth wood and placed her hands in the holes on either side. She wondered just how many other necks had rested here. Hale lowered the beam over the nape of her neck and secured the device. Harriet immediately felt physical discomfort. She was standing, bent forward, her head at waist height, her hips taking the strain. She shuffled her feet, flexed her wrists and attempted to rotate her head. There was no way she could pull free.

Hale was stand in front of her, assessing the device with a scholarly eye. His erection showed no signs of receding. If anything, it was more pronounced.

'Well,' Harriet teased, eying the swelling, 'What are you going to do to me?'

'It's about time I got my own back,' he replied, a note of glee in his voice.

He moved behind Harriet and she sensed he was standing very close. She imagined his eyes roaming across her body. In this strange position, she felt very vulnerable. She trembled in anticipation. In a second, he hitched her skirt up and planted his hands on her exposed rump, a warm palm clasping each plump cheek, smoothing her prickling flesh. Harriet didn't resist. The young professor massaged her bottom lightly, strong fingers digging gently but firmly into the supple tissue. He was taking his time, sizing her up. He kneaded and squeezed, his hands rotating wantonly, thumbs trailing over the gusset of her skimpy pink knickers, pushing the fabric deep into the cleft, easing the silky satin up her back, rendering more bare skin to his determined touch.

She closed her eyes, savoured the resolute strumming of his fingers, a light tap and then – Ow! – a single smack. Her body jolted forward, an involuntary reaction to the suddenness of the slap rather than any physical pain. Her skin buzzed.

She felt so naughty; she was far too old to be spanked. But she liked it. She liked it a lot. He slapped her butt again, this time more forcefully. Harriet flinched, savouring the brief sting and then the sizzling rush. Her bottom, momentarily cool, now flushed red-hot. It was not alone; her pussy was hungrily devouring the pain of pleasure. It craved attention. It ached to be filled.

'Fuck me!' Harriet cried out, spreading her taut, stretched legs apart.

Hale wasted no time, wrenching the crotch of her damp panties to one side. His first thrust opened her up pleasingly. His second, harder and deeper, made her gasp. His hands remained firmly clenched to her butt as he thrust in and out, penetrating her further with every long stroke. Harriet felt her orgasm grow rapidly. She clenched her fists and closed her eyes, held Hale's pounding muscle tight, her cunt rippling joyously over the firm shaft. With a final thrust, he came inside her and her knees buckled.

Standing at the front door of the museum, the breeze still whistling through the courtyard, Harriet no longer felt cold.

Party Of The Third Part
by Jeremy Edwards

I think we were in the kitchen, cleaning up after dinner on a weeknight, when Margaret broached the subject. 'Julia wants to watch us,' was what she said.

Julia was Margaret's best friend – *our* best friend, really, by this point. Though Margaret's statement was out of the blue and, on the surface, rather vague, I tingled with a hunch. 'Watch us?' I replied. I poured myself a little more of the Pinot Noir that I'd retrieved from the dining-room table.

Margaret blushed slightly as our eyes met. 'Yeah. She wants to – you know – watch us do it. I think she's bored.'

I laughed. 'She wants to watch us 'do it' because she's *bored*? How bored can you get?'

Margaret smiled, but her explanation was in earnest. 'She's still between relationships, taking some time to re-acquaint herself with herself, keeping a low profile.' Margaret and Julia had eaten lunch together the day before. Since both Margaret and I had been out of the house till late in the evening that day, this was the first I'd heard about their lunchtime chat. It seems the best conversations always happen when I can't attend a get-together.

'Anyway . . . she told me she's not really ready to go out looking for sex again. But I guess she's becoming weary of the same old auto-eroticism scene. That's why she asked if she could come over and watch us sometime.'

Margaret made it sound so simple, so logical. Yet I couldn't help laughing again. 'You surprise me, sweetcheeks. From what I've been reading lately, masturbation is practically the hottest sex out there for the sensuous woman.'

My wife smirked, mischievously this time. She reached forward to poke my taut belly. 'Who says it isn't? But, just for a change of scene, Julia wants to come over and masturbate in our bedroom. With *us* heating it up.'

Call me dense, but it hadn't yet occurred to me that lovely Julia would actually be masturbating while she watched us 'do it'. Margaret's eyes travelled down my body as the front of my trousers grew un-mysteriously full and hard. Half an hour later, she was riding me for all she was worth and having the most intense orgasm she'd experienced in weeks.

Julia was wearing a shoulder-teasing sun dress when she arrived for dinner. Her fresh-featured expression and corn-blonde hair were topped off with an elegant straw hat. The hat, I was pleased to find, remained on during the meal.

Julia was not more beautiful, nor more charming, nor more sexy than my Margaret. But she was the only woman I knew who came close in all categories. I imagine many men have a two-women-in-bed fantasy; and in my fantasy life, there was no question that the party of the third part was our friend Julia. Margaret knew this, and she was perfectly comfortable with it. So comfortable, in fact, that she had acted like I was doing *her* a favour when I'd joined in assenting to Julia's request.

The meal was less leisurely than it had been on the many previous occasions on which Julia had been our guest. We

98

all seemed to be honouring an unspoken arrangement to keep things moving swiftly along.

'I think dessert later, probably,' said Margaret, looking to me for feedback.

'Definitely,' I said. My mind had already moved beyond food.

'I hope you really don't mind my 'tagging along' into the bedroom tonight,' said Julia. 'I was the kid sister in my family, so I guess tagging along is in my blood.' Her sensitively-moulded face favoured us with one of its most engaging grins. She looked positively kissable.

Margaret beamed back at her, indulgently. 'Don't worry.'

I felt myself harden as we all silently acknowledged each other's complicity.

In the bedroom, I was a little self-conscious at first – despite my dining-room erection. It felt strange to know that Julia was watching while I gave Margaret's luscious, bare ass an inaugural squeeze and I delivered a kiss to each hind cheek. Margaret, however, showed no signs of awkwardness.

Taking my cue from her, I too relaxed. Quickly warming to the situation, I gave Margaret's behind more kisses and squeezes.

Out of the corner of my eye, I could see Julia. She was sitting in her sun dress and floppy hat in a comfortable chair, her thighs spread just enough for me to glimpse her pink panties. Her sensual mouth was open.

With Margaret's bottom wiggling delectably, I could already tell that she was in the mood to be taken doggie-style tonight. Though neither of us was quite ready, she previewed the main attraction by getting up on her knees and offering herself to me, rear first. With her derriere in my face, I kissed her soft pussy lips, licking and tasting, until she was quivering.

99

As I removed my mouth from my wife's wet love-hole, something in my peripheral vision caught my attention. I turned my head for an instant, long enough to see that Julia had slipped a finger into her panties. Her body was rocking gracefully, and her kissable lips were pouting intently.

I knew that Margaret would probably want another helping of foreplay. In this spirit, I decided to drive her wild by further stimulating her erogenous zones. With nimble deftness, my tickle finger jumped from the crack of her tingling ass to the place she likes it under her arm . . . then back again.

'Oh, yeah, tickle her ass,' said a voice behind me. I turned my head again and saw Julia gazing at us with a milky, drunken look. Her panties were stretched to the limit and her hand was jammed in there, working herself like crazy. Her knees were even vibrating.

A blissful 'ooh' from Margaret brought my attention back to where it primarily belonged. I knew this body so well, and I could tell just from the rhythm of its undulations, and the temperature and firmness of the flesh I was currently kneading, that it was time. I reached under Margaret's chest and embraced her in an intimate hug, my hands softly groping her breasts and my engorged cock pressing against the crack of her bottom. Before entering her sweet little cunt from behind, I gave it a few strokes with my fingers, teasing the lips and spreading the fresh juices that even Julia could probably smell.

Margaret and I sank forward as I thrust into her. While we pounded against each other, I once again titillated the sensitive flesh under her arms.

I heard Julia cry out in glee when I came. Moments later, with my hand and her own working her clit as a practiced team, Margaret shuddered around my numbness. We collapsed in a heap, and she kissed her pillow as the delirious aftershocks rippled through her.

Dessert was anti-climactic. Julia and Margaret made plans to have lunch together again, and the conversation drifted into upcoming concerts and vacations.

When Julia bent to collect her tote bag prior to leaving, I noticed the clinging wet stain on the underside of her panties.

'She wants to do it again,' Margaret said over supper, after she'd next seen Julia. 'We were thinking this Friday.'

We were thinking this Friday. I noted that there was no doubt in any of our minds that the arrangement would be agreeable. It was merely a question of what day would work.

Margaret and I had been fucking with even less inhibition than usual since Julia had watched us. Tonight, fresh from our discussion about the next session, we practically ground the mattress into the floor.

Margaret and I had already undressed when Julia suggested a variation.

'How would you feel if I were closer this time?' she asked. 'The bed is pretty big… I thought maybe I could sit at the edge and watch from there.' Before we had even answered, Julia was sitting, tentatively, at the corner of the bed, testing its bounce. She looked like a hotel guest who has yet to discard her shoes and freshen up, but who wants to sample the inviting mattress before doing anything else.

Margaret and I exchanged glances. Her half-nod of hopeful encouragement, along with her trademark indulgent smile, confirmed that she and I were on the same page.

'Make yourself at home,' I said to Julia.

I dived onto the fitted sheet with Margaret. I was totally naked; she was nude except for the no-longer-closed front-closing bra that flapped enticingly around as I licked at her nipples. It was a bit surreal doing all this with Julia seated

101

neatly at the edge of the bed – dressed elegantly in a skirt, a floral blouse, and stockings. But though it was weird, it was also a turn-on – for me, certainly, and for Margaret as well, I could assume. When I thrust my arm between Margaret's legs and rubbed her pussy with my wrist, Julia's slender fingers darted neatly up her own skirt. And when I began fingering Margaret's asshole, I noticed Julia's breasts pressing discreetly against her blouse.

Cock entered cunt, slowly, and I now held Margaret's arms gently above her, opening her body to all the pleasure that my mouth could deliver across her torso while the pulse of my prick throbbed through her interior. Julia's rear began to bounce sympathetically on the mattress she'd tested earlier.

'Put your finger back in her ass,' Julia urged.

'Hey, no comments from the peanut gallery.' It just felt like the thing for me to say. After all, Margaret seemed happy – to say the least – as we were, and, well, a guy only has two hands.

I saw Julia grin at my retort. I observed that she had her right hand around the back of her skirt, under which she had presumably found her own anus to tease. At the front, her plump pussy lips flashed us as they enjoyed the full attention of her left hand. Stockings, yes; panties, no, I realised. She looked gorgeously lewd, doing herself in both holes.

A shout of acute bliss from Margaret turned my eyes back her way, and soon we were trembling together. The bed bounced emphatically when Julia writhed to her private climax, her digits frenetically active.

By the third Friday evening, we had settled into a routine. Margaret and I cooked, and Julia brought the wine.

As dinner wound down, I could see that Julia was getting wound up. Again, she raised the subject of ground rules.

'I know I'm here only as an observer. But I was wondering...' she began, tentatively. 'I was wondering if I need to remain dressed this time. And if it would be OK if I... if I...' she lowered her eyes; was she actually blushing? 'If I touched you both,' she finished.

'You want to touch us?' Margaret, too, looked flushed – and intrigued.

'Yes, Margaret, I want to touch you, while you . . . do it,' Julia averred. 'Maybe be touched by you, too, especially when I'm . . . getting close.' Her eyes now met mine directly.

The implications of Julia's proposal, and the delicate way she had delivered it, were making me predictably horny. Yet I was confused. 'If you actually get undressed,' I said, 'and touch us, and are touched by us, and are brought to orgasm . . . in what way, exactly, are you just an 'observer'?'

'It's all in the attitude,' Julia answered, with a return of her poise. 'I will maintain a detached, aloof attitude.'

I raised an eyebrow. 'Do you expect us to buy that?'

'No,' she admitted graciously.

That night, Julia reclined on our bed, enjoying a nudity that suggested oil paintings. Her hand felt sweet on my thigh as I pumped into Margaret. Margaret, in turn, clasped her friend's other hand in a tender grip, even when orgasm claimed them both. The picture was completed by the presence of my fingers just inside the lips of Julia's cunt, where she gyrated around my passive presence. With minimal help from me, she coaxed herself first to dampness and finally to climax.

Another week passed, and Julia arrived for dinner with more wine . . . and more boldness.

'OK,' she said over salad. 'Who am I kidding. I want to hop in the sack with you two and have it all.'

103

'I guess this was inevitable,' Margaret laughed, her eyes twinkling.

As the three of us undressed, I felt like we were on a swim team. But I knew I was getting ready for something better than a swim meet.

Julia was the first to break the ice. 'Do me a favour,' she requested of me. 'Give my ass cheeks a couple of little slaps. They're itching for it.' She pointed her enticing bottom my way and sent a hand into her own crotch. Margaret nodded to me, and I complied, relishing Julia's wiggles and giggles beneath my gentle palm. Within seconds, the hand she had wedged into herself brought forth a playful climax.

'That's what I've been missing,' she said. 'It gets lonely back there when I go too long without some friendly stimulation.'

A few minutes later, I found myself lifting the topsheet so that it covered two sets of feminine legs to the back of the thigh, with the result that two lovely bottoms were framed above the border of the sheet. Where my Margaret's had a quiet, statuesque grace, Julia's boasted a winking sexuality. Its modest roundness drew the eye in from the streamlined territory of her petite, milk-white back.

I could not keep my hands off either of these glorious derrieres. I was tempted to climb atop them and grind myself against the cheeks, rolling from one behind to the other, until I should orgasm all over the inviting flesh.

Something flashed through my mind. *'Put your finger back in her ass.'* Julia from the peanut gallery, two weeks earlier, when her participation in our lovemaking had been indirect. And so, in the midst of stroking my wife's cunt lips with my left hand, I placed the tip of my right forefinger in our friend Julia's tidy asshole. It made me incredibly aroused to see them both wriggle beneath me. My wife's brown hair and Julia's blonde hair were twin manes of dynamic sexuality as they pressed their hot faces into their respective pillows.

When I saw a hand touching Julia's cunt, I initially thought it was her own. Then I realised it was Margaret's, and this realization further augmented my erection.

I flopped on top of them, still keeping one hand in Margaret's cunt and the other in Julia's rear. We formed a sort of flattened, rudimentary human pyramid, a jiggling pile of flesh that was awake to all pleasures. My head was level with their shoulder blades, and my rigid cock pushed deliciously into the crevice formed where their thighs pressed together. The soft flesh on either side of my member formed a metaphorical cunt; and, while I kissed their dainty backs and tickled their orifices, I felt like I was fucking a new, abstract woman, a collage of flesh and scent and sensation into which my wife and our friend had merged. Even the sounds they made began to blend . . . so that instead of hearing Margaret's happy whimpers on my left and Julia's intense moans on my right, I began to hear a musical composite, in which it became difficult to distinguish the individual voices. This choral effect gave a transcendent, sublime quality to the entire sensory experience, and when their orgasms triggered my own I felt like I was having a dream – a wet dream.

Margaret got up to pee, and Julia headed for the living room. I thought we might be finished for the evening. But then Julia came back, still beautifully nude, with a fresh bottle of wine. And as she returned from a second trip – with glasses and a corkscrew – Margaret emerged from the bathroom, sighing with the synergistic contentment of orgasm followed by bathroom break.

Julia held the wine bottle up. It was a luscious prop in the hands of such a sexual creature. 'Will you join me?' she asked with a slight formality that seemed humorously out of place, under the circumstances.

The rich red glasses of Cabernet must have looked striking against our three pale bodies, as we sat comfortably on the bed.

'You guys are just great,' said Julia, her face glowing from a quickly-consumed gulp of wine. 'There's no married couple I'd rather go to bed with.'

'I'll take that as a compliment,' said Margaret with a chuckle.

Julia wasn't laughing, though. She was sincerely affectionate, and she leaned in to give Margaret a hug. I got my hug, in turn, a moment later. Not sure where to go from there, I hugged Margaret. This time, all three of us chuckled.

Over the wine, we gushed about how great it was to have friends one could feel so close to, be so naked with.

When the wine was all gone, Julia put her hand in my crotch. 'Could you fuck me, Bertie?' Before I could answer, she turned to Margaret. 'Can Bertie fuck me?'

I smiled at them. '*Can* I? Or *may* I?' I looked down into my lap, where I could detect a stirring of dormant flesh. 'It looks like I *can*'

Margaret kissed me sensuously on the lips. 'And you *may*,' she said. 'We did tell Julia she could have it all, remember.' The wine on my wife's breath smelled like love and generosity.

Julia wasn't kidding. She lay down, sprawling, her pussy an invitation. Margaret gently pushed me toward her, urging me on with giggles.

I nibbled my way up Julia's torso, from just above her fair-haired mound to the crook between her breasts. I placed two tentative hands on her chest and leaned my face in, wondering if she would like to be kissed . . . or simply fucked. She suddenly popped her head up and took the initiative, giving me a sassy kiss that tasted like tipsy daring.

She was so ready for me that I almost didn't notice her sliding my cock inside her. But the velvety warmth soon awoke all my nerves down there. I saw her shoulders dance against the bed beneath me, and I felt her inner womanhood melt around me.

'Go on, my darling,' a most familiar voice whispered from behind. 'Fuck her in your best style.' Margaret's palm was on my butt cheek. Her fingers were trembling with excitement.

It all happened so fast that it was, in a way, hard to believe afterwards that it had really happened at all. However, the scream of joyous release in my ear and the clenching, raw gift of a friend's pussy were too vivid to be products of my imagination. As my come shot out of me, I felt that I had consecrated a tender friendship in a way that would enrich all our lives for ever, even if it were never repeated.

I wanted to fuck Margaret next, but I was tired, she was tired . . . we were all tired. Julia fell asleep in Margaret's arms. They looked like sisters now. I joined them under the quilt, feeling a sort of fulfilment that was not quite like anything I'd ever known before, even in a life full of happy feelings.

'What happens next week?' Margaret and I wondered in the morning. But Julia had already decided.

On the following Friday, she sat near us on the bed, dressed again (but with her pussy visible at key moments). She got herself off within inches of us, but she didn't touch us.

On the Friday after that, she sat in the armchair across the room and kept her panties on. She brought herself to climax through her silk.

On the next Friday after, she invited herself to dinner but made it clear it was for dinner only.

Julia's involvement in our lovemaking proved to have been like the moon waxing and waning through a single cycle . . . or like a roller-coaster's parabola.

The friendship never diminished – it became, in fact, richer, deeper, and more joyous than ever – but her presence as a guest was more irregular. Before long she found herself a splendid boyfriend. Margaret and I always love giving them dinner – after which they trundle home to enjoy each other in private, while Margaret and I do the same here.

The ripples from the sexual splash that Julia made in our lives have yet to vanish, though it's been years now. Margaret and I agree that our intimate moments have been that much more mind-blowing since those unforgettable Friday nights.

And once in a while, when I'm nuzzling into Margaret on the bed . . . perhaps just beginning to kiss her neck or fondle her bottom or grope her crotch . . . she whispers, 'Let's pretend Julia's watching.'

Prima Volta Del Samantha
by Avi Moskovitz & Conrad Lawrence

Any hope of being swept off her feet set with the sun slipping off the far edge of the flat plain of Chicago. Framed in the pane of her window more than twenty floors above that metropolitan plane, she peered through her own translucent face, reflecting a dull pragmatic reality. The best she might ever expect from a man would be someone... different.

Perhaps, by lowering her expectations, an incredible experience could be shared with a man of a typical nature. She closed her laptop, closing down another solitary workday executed at her office/dining room table. Prince Charming had not called for a date. Hell, Prince Charming didn't even have her number... Still, someone had called and just having someone to meet meant breaking up her solitary routine of waking, walking the dogs, working, walking the dogs, lunching, working, walking...

Samantha sighed. Once there had been a time when prepping for a date had been exciting, filled with pampering and anticipation, luscious self-touching, self-denying anticipation. This evening, though, the memory of all the recent romance-challenged, post-relationship underdogs who'd paraded her through a variety of unimpressive restaurants and self-indulgent conversations caused her to speak aloud with no one to hear her. 'For once, could someone at least impress me by having some interest in me, beyond what kind of lingerie I wear. Take some interest in my hopes; or at least be so good-looking as to excuse the testosterone-driven self consciousness.'

Ensconced in post-Blackberry recall technology, the address of a restaurant oozed to the surface of her Palm as disappointment sunk deeper into the largest organ of stimulation she possessed, her mind. Family dining did not bode well for romantic impressiveness, though she had to say it qualified as unique. 'You owe me one, brother dear.'

Newest attorney at her brother's power-litigating firm had a nice ring of potential to it, so during the date setting phone conversations, she had ignored the father of five aspect hiding behind the curtain of reality. Seeing the choice of restaurant somehow parted that curtain, with images of kids banging utensils on glasses and conversations peppered with parental admonishments. Samantha soaped her breasts trying to sponge away the sense of obligation and frustration, hardening her nipples, letting them swell with that old anticipatory hope. The glass door steamed up, wrapping her into her a familiar world of sensual gratification, fulfilment cascading down her in a hot spray; a world that swirled down the shower drain.

Oh well, a prematurely ending date would leave her out of the house and sexied up. Why not take all that repressed sexual energy and inflict a bit of simpatico torment on the hoard of carnally deluded males swarming the throbbing hip hop clubs. Who knows? If dancing didn't suffice to quell hormonal frustration, then one might prove interesting enough to be allowed to intrude on her night. Interesting enough to be allowed to peel off the cashmere turtleneck, grey wool skirt, thigh-high black lace, flower-patterned stockings, and black lace bra; all fitting so tightly they might have been brushed on her by the stroke of the artist.

110

Sexy, sophisticated, yet edgy; Samantha grabbed a cab, struggling to hold onto sophistication or at least edginess, fighting the gravity of impending disappointment. I am on time. I look amazing. With confident elegant strides I will make an entrance and turn every male head in this restaurant. Well, at least the heads of every male above the age of ten.

Before reaching the door, a man wearing a grey cashmere overcoat and tightly woven tweed scarf stepped out of the recesses; either from her mind or an adjoining doorway. 'Excuse me, Samantha? Are you Samantha Rose?'

The most incredible man with wavy black hair, blue eyes and a strong chin occluded everything else along Michigan Avenue, his stunning, tall, Italian virility exuded strength and control. 'Why, yes, I am. Why do you ask?'

'I am Ray LaRosa and I am supposed to meet Samantha Lambkin here.'

Alive with an infusion of difference, she gazed on a man any woman would gladly allow to father a whole tribe. She looked away from the aqua blue eyes which she wished only to swim within, as if they were warm Caribbean waters, searching for signs of his children. Reality rose to hopeful expectation. None were visible.

'I am Samantha.'

One hand, so large and strong that Samantha yearned to be taken within his grasp, extended to her. 'Great! Your brother doesn't do you justice, but then what brother does? I cannot believe that an incredibly beautiful woman such as you has not been swept off her feet into marriage! Such is my great luck. I can see I'll have my work cut out to make it to date two!'

His soft warm hand enveloped hers, her soul. Though possessing an outdoorsman's build, his touch betrayed hours spent in an office.

111

His second hand gracefully reached out, covering both their hands, holding them both in a world of their own, one of those worlds created under the privacy of a quilt. Did he pull her closer, or had she moved of her own volition? He smiled. 'I have a car coming for us. I only asked you to meet me here because it's an easy place to find and I needed to be sure you were really OK with the concept of dating a father of five. I hope you are also OK about surprises.'

An inner calm radiated into Samantha through his touch, assuaging any hesitation she felt. She was not in the grip of a common or garden conservative lawyer-father. No. This creature transcended any concept of male she had previously conjured up. She surrendered herself to surprise. Maintaining both a physical and cerebral hold, Ray conveyed the sense that his attention was completely absorbed by her, even while his eyes moved.

He doted on her, placing her in the limo that appeared at the curb, as if she were a Fabergé egg, settling her safely into the seat. A tropical humidity warmed her at the thought of kissing Ray, the anticipation of feeling hard muscles against her bare breasts, coiling in his arms after a long deep tryst. Never before had she been taken by someone with such immediacy, such urgency.

She wanted to make love to him right at that moment; but how to signal to him and maintain her signature sophistication and elegant grace? Had she worn a button-down blouse, she could have opened another button, signalling her surrender. Such an odd conundrum, usually she found herself fighting off a lecherous onslaught, not seeking to expedite it.

Though he entered from the other side of the limo, Ray sat close enough for Samantha to feel the warmth he exuded. She sidled closer so that her contact with him became more than a light touch, but an actual press.

The usual routine of surrender would be far from routine with this man she knew. Samantha would have been delighted simply taking Ray home to her bed. Usually, she had to be unclothed with someone physically fawning over to feel the level of sexual arousal she felt now, the deep wetness that filled her as well as the feeling of being so hooked into Ray, as if they had been lovers for ever. She did not want to waste time with dinner; she could have gone right to her place and gotten lost in the evening.

So absorbed was she in Ray, Samantha took no note of their destination or the time it took to get there. Ray drew her out of her seat with the same strong gentle grip that drew out the need to kiss him. Standing, she did not release him, but pulled him to her, brushing the lobe of his ear with her lips. 'Thank you for making our blind date so special.'

Brushing her lips along his cheek, Samantha likewise brushed a nipple aching for release from her sweater along his arm, then to ensure Ray would understand her attraction to him and trust for his plans, she pressed her breast against him. Rarely, if ever, did a man impress Samantha enough to be so floridly forward.

Somehow she knew Ray to be capable of raising the sexual tension of the night while still encouraging intimacy. He'd already ensured a second date. A welcoming smile, a bowl filled with the ripe cherries of seduction, spread across his face. 'Samantha, be yourself tonight and do not hold back. I am hoping to draw something out of you that perhaps you didn't know existed.'

Both hope and the expectant kiss hung in the air, leaving Samantha incensed at her inability to engage Ray and her immediate desire to succumb to him. She felt what? Rejected? No! Challenged! Challenged in the most dichotomous way: her inability to manipulate this man into taking control of her, of imposing his masculine essence on her feminine self.

The epitome of chivalry, Ray opened a door. 'I just need to get a gift for the party. Do you mind helping me pick it out?'

Samantha passed through the door Ray held open for her, finding herself in a world of fine lingerie: La Perla, her favourite. What kind of party required lingerie? Samantha's pulse rate and ardour rose. She bobbed in a sea of lingerie swimming in Ray's aura of appreciation, the knowledge that together they posed a striking image. Men in the store smiled at Samantha, winked at Ray, sharks in warm friendly waters, the waters of a stranger. 'Do you,' Ray spoke into her hair, 'have a suggestion?'

Surprise pulled Samantha toward the safety of full-length nightgowns, propelled by the conundrum of not wanting to give the wrong impression, yet wanting to reveal her wild spirit yearning for release. She plucked three silk and satin gowns from their perches, eyeing Ray for approval. He smiled and nodded toward the dressing rooms. She eyed the sales person for permission. The woman's smile and nod mirrored Ray's.

Eyeing herself in the dressing room mirror, Samantha couldn't help wonder what Ray's reaction might be at the sight of her thighs through the slit plackets of the first gown. Her hand parted the placket, slipping up along her inner thigh, following her stomach, cupping and fondling her breast. Would Ray's enormous hands follow that same path? Were the view in the mirror his, would it pique his manhood? Her eyes closed, shutting out the distraction of his absence. Would he speak? Loudly or in...

A whisper behind her, husky and virile, spoke. 'Nice'

She opened her eyes. Ray didn't just look at her. He drank her in, his savouring adoration warming the chill of surprise. Samantha turned to Ray, searching deep in his adoration for approval, willing to submit to being wrapped in that admiration. A moist fever spread down the insides of

114

her thigh the same way a desire to be closer, to beckon touch, spread through her, but she didn't want make to the first move. No. She needed to be taken. Ray denied her, leaving her suspended in uncomfortable silence. 'Please leave me, so I can try the next gown.'

Surprised by the husky quality her voice had taken and suddenly alone in her memory of it, Samantha draped herself in the next gown. Less silk, more lace, more flesh prompted her to reach for the matching robe. 'Come, Ray. Would you like to feel... the fabric?' she called and held out her arm and the silk.

Ray entered and reached to her, his hand extending not toward her sleeve, but toward her breasts. Samantha drew in a breath, waiting in fearful hope. Ray took the fabric that caressed the inside curve of her breast between thumb and forefinger. He denied her full satisfaction again, his hand rising to her shoulder. Appreciative eyes coupled, acknowledging the feint and the parry.

Determined to make the pursuit worth his while, Samantha's hand brushed the lace along her stomach with her fingertips, as if reading it like some erotic Braille that would tell her the next move. The movement captured Ray's eyes, following her hand to thigh, then back up to breasts.

Still, Ray did not make an advance. Damn his will. He defers his gratification, striving for something better.

Samantha looked away, her own image in the mirror peering back at her. The innocence of the moment had passed. Animal passion overrode guileless deference. Hands pressed on Ray's chest, Samantha leaned into him and a deep kiss. Large strong hands clamped her wrists, pulling them behind her; a control hold. She struggled to break free by pressing her torso to him, an unsuccessful attempt to break his grip. His strength didn't falter. She released a perfectly timed involuntary whimper, a beckoning wince. Ray released her, his grasp lingering with a gentle kiss on the lips. 'I'm sorry. I hope that I didn't hurt you.'

Deft hands and empathetic eyes drew a forgiving, responsive, kiss from Samantha, returned with a gentle flattening of her breasts against his chest. Tit for tat, Samantha held the kiss until she felt him relax, then bit his lip. Both drew back, looking for blood. Samantha suddenly became aware of the beat of her heart. The stakes for the evening had been raised. 'Get out so I can try on the next gown,' Samantha admonished.

Hell hath no fury.

Ray should not have denied her.

With nipple-hardening anticipation, Samantha feared retribution. Ray left, obediently, only to return with fervour as she laced up her shoes, throwing aside the dressing curtain, towering over her, an ensemble of garters, lace stocking, bra and thong held out; not so much as a tithe, but more like a demand. Dropping them on the bench, he cupped her under the shoulders, lifting her to him, penetrating her lips with a deep demanding passion. Thankful that he held her, keeping her head above the surface of her swirling desire, she said, 'I – I thought you wanted to go.'

'Try this on!' He left, leaving her hanging on the residual memory of his grip. He'd not asked. For that very reason, Samantha considered not putting on the ensemble, but she wanted him, wanted to feel his hands on her, wanted to be taken; but on her own terms.

She considered waiting for him, without wearing a single stitch of clothing; considered whether that would be surrender or domination. Surely, the surrender of herself would hold some power over Ray, some force that would break his will to deny her the satisfaction a man like him could give her. Surely, this denial of her must be a denial of self for him. Surely, he must want her as much as she wanted him.

As if donning a life vest to keep her afloat in a churning carnal sea, Samantha put on the outfit Ray had thrust at her, knowing full well that she had already gone overboard; treading water, waiting for rescue from her own craving.

The weave of each article clung to her as if an extension of the sexual perfection she felt. Did she exude that sexual excellence into the clinging fibres? Or did she draw it from the expensive fabric that cupped her breasts like shielding hands, the thin cords wrapped around her hips? They provided a minimally protective pouch for lips aching for Ray's touch, perhaps violation, but at her moment of choosing.

'Ray?'

Ray entered, his mouth frozen open in unrequited speech. Samantha looked into his eyes, the power of vulnerability becoming clear to her. Standing before him with little more than dainty patches of fine fabric covering her, she held some power over him. Looking away from his eyes would mean breaking the lock she held over him, but she had to see to what extent she affected him.

The strain against the front of his trousers indicated that Ray had more than enough potential to be a satisfying lover. More to maintain her empowerment, rather than to give it over to Ray by revealing her desire, Samantha peered through the fog of sexual tension that had condensed in the room. Ray bit his lip, reaching for her breast with spread fingers.

Perfect!

He wanted to touch her. Samantha wanted to feel his touch. The move appeared involuntary, as if outside Ray's control. Samantha pushed past his reach, placing her breasts where she, not he, desired, flattening them against his chest, her lips beside his ear. 'I have to buy this outfit – and wear

117

it out of here. I can't let the sales girl touch it and discover how wet I am.'

'Hmmmm,' Ray cooed. 'Is it the outfit that makes you wet or...' Samantha clamped his earlobe in her teeth, snipping his sentence. His rhetoric changed. 'I'm glad we agree. This is precisely the kind of gift I was seeking.'

Ray tried to pull back, but Samantha held the lobe of his ear firm. With the barest of winces escaping from his machismo, Ray realised he'd been trapped. Samantha felt him tense, then relax. He wedged his hand between them, fingers stretching up just under her breasts. Samantha pulled him closer, giving him no opportunity to find something for pinching, a tender nipple, in return, though the possibility possessed a certain allure. Surrender. Control. Pleasure. Pain. The choices blurred. Samantha released his lobe, pressing a tongue in his ear, feeling the mounting tension in his arm relax, then gripped the lobe of his ear again.

Ray seemed to surrender, leaning to her with the weight of his full six-foot-plus virility, but she could feel him hold himself, and her, away from the wall behind her. Fear seeped out of her mind, flowing down through her, pooling moistly in the depths of her sexuality, tingling in electric anticipation at the extreme surfaces of her most sensitive places. Ray could pin her to the wall, but he didn't. Why? Her fear deepened; a penetrating, yearning fear. His hands busied themselves behind her. She could feel it through the rolling movement of his muscles under the skin of his shoulders.

She pressed her hips against him, finding the hard bulge of his waning discipline. Even through his pants she felt his fever. Then he collapsed, falling against her, pressing her to the wall. His hand reached behind him, quickly, grabbing her arms; pulling them up, entwining her wrists in soft, liquid satin. Samantha's mind wrapped itself in the soft woolly realization that Ray's surrender had been a feint. While she had luxuriated in the pleasure of having him in her grip, he'd tied a sash from one of the robes to the clothes hook above her head. The loops he formed in the sash tightened around her wrists, pulling them above her head, lashing them to the hook. So exposed, nothing she could do could stop Ray from touching her in any way he wanted.

A visceral agitation filled Samantha, simultaneously burning and blowing through her like a sub-zero wind. Ray stepped back, leaving a dreadful certainty that he would once again deny Samantha. He dropped his cashmere coat to the floor, sweeping Samantha with hungry eyes of victory. Fear burned as the blue core in the orange flame of determination heated the moment to urgency. Samantha need to decide if her need lay in succumbing or resisting.

Some instinct, surged through the surface of Samantha's consciousness. She wanted Ray, but she wanted him on her own terms. Whatever it was that surged from deep within took control of her. Grasping the hook above her head, she brought her legs up, wrapping her thighs around Ray's neck, dropping her calves over his shoulders, then under his arms.

She held him.

In his struggles, Samantha felt a strength, the kind of strength that she both desired and feared, between her legs. She held him, till he calmed; peering at her over the mound of her thong, past her stomach, which was heaving more from anticipation than exertion. The mutual acknowledgement, in their moment of impasse in their gaze, gripped them both in something stronger than she'd shared with a man she'd let enter her. Already, Samantha felt a climax mounting deep within.

'Untie my hands.'

Ray smiled. He denied her again. Anger rushed through Samantha. Ray shouldn't have denied her.

Samantha arched her back, pulling her calves toward her, drawing Ray's mouth so close to the mound protected by the sparse fabric of her thong that she could feel the humidity of his breath adding to her own moist heat. Their eyes locked. She thrust at Ray's mouth in that begging, demanding way the body has when it takes over control and seeks release and satisfaction. Ray struggled, pulling back, trying to free himself; a silent struggle for they knew that too much noise could bring unwelcome participants to this tryst, such as the police.

Samantha's legs ached, not in the same way as her need ached, but the ache of fatigue. Ray's strength would wear her down and her need for release would break her concentration.

Samantha gave up on intellectualising her way through her predicament and let some forgotten animalistic sense take over. She threw herself into a frenzy, thrusting at Ray's face, hard enough that her mound rubbed against his chin and mouth, barely protected by the thin fabric that covered her. Arousal drove her fury, subsiding only partly at the realization that she had brought the exquisite Italian stud to his knees, causing him to pant his words, 'OK. OK.'

Trembling, on the cusp of release, yet not satisfied, Samantha looked down, past her heaving breasts, at the man she held in a trembling grasp between her legs. What, she wondered caused the trembling? fatigue? or a mounting climax that she almost feared because her need for it had become so strong? Hands tied to a hook in the wall, she held at her disposal the most incredible man she'd ever laid eyes on.

'Do not deny me!'

With a look that Samantha couldn't quite identify, Ray's hands slid up around her hips, pulling the thong to one side,

allowing him to bring his lips to her fevered swollen labia.
Words escaped her in deep gasps.

'Do as I say!'

Ray nodded.

'Tongue me.'

Ray's tongue parted the folds of her lips

'Stroke my nipples.'

Ray's hands rose up along her stomach, cupping her
breasts, pulling down the bra; alternately flicking each
nipple with a strong finger, then deftly stroking the sides of
them with his thumb and rolling them between thumb and
forefinger. Samantha shuddered, the mound between her
legs vibrating against Ray's lips

'Lick my clit.'

The tip of Ray's tongue ran up the full length of her lips,
searching under the little hood, finding that swollen button
of flesh, ready to explode.

'Suck on it.'

Ray drew Samantha's clit into his mouth, then released
it. Flicked it with his tongue, then drew it in again,
repeating, perhaps knowing that Samantha would issue no
more commands; only pleading, mounting moans that
would soon erupt in screams.

When Samantha reached that eruption, Ray rose up,
filling her. His mouth over hers, he swallowed her screams,
enough so that the clerks might not hear. Wave after wave
of climax flowed through Samantha as she thrust against his
rock-hard desire for her, absorbing his own spasms of
release. When their mutual climaxes had finally subsided,
they clung to each other, for long moments, gasping for
breath, grasping for a hold on the real world.

Gazing into each others eyes, as Samantha had with
other lovers, yet not with the same knowledge that
something profound had been shared, Ray found words
first.

'Well, that certainly was different!'

Stocking Fetish
by Eva Hore

My flat mate Sarah and I have a great relationship. We tell each other everything, which is why I came to wonder what she was up to when I *accidentally* saw all these sexy stockings and underwear, in her bedroom drawer. OK, I admit it. I was snooping. Anyway, she'd met this new guy, Ricky, and was very secretive about him. She was hardly ever home now so when I heard that he had to stay over for the weekend while his house was being painted, I was pleased I'd finally get to meet him.

The problem was though, that she wouldn't share him. Wouldn't even let me talk to him. They locked themselves up in her bedroom, hardly came out at all. Intrigued, I decided to spy on them. They rushed out to have dinner at some fancy restaurant. Sarah was wearing the highest heels I've ever seen, fish-net stockings, and a red leather, skin-tight dress.

I decided to plant my video camera on a tripod at her bedroom window. It had a remote control panel, so after hooking it into my television, I waited anxiously for their return. Sarah and I had talked often about our sexual fantasies and discussed boyfriends truthfully, which was why I was so annoyed that she wouldn't tell me anything about Ricky. The longer I sat and wondered, the more my mind wandered, until I was desperate for some action. Fortunately I didn't have too long to wait. They burst through her bedroom door, their hands all over each other. He whipped off her dress and threw it to the floor.

Fuck! I've seen her nearly naked before, coming in and out of the shower but never like this. She was fucking gorgeous. She had on a black leather garter belt which had her fish-net stockings hooked into it, a tiny matching G-string, that hugged the crack of her sexy arse, and this absolutely hot push-up bra that had her tits practically spilling out of their cups.

She was taller than him in her stilettos and he pushed her up against her bedroom door, ravishing her body with kisses. He worked his way down, pulling her tits from their cups so they hung over where he suckled at her breasts. Then he was inching his way down, kissing her everywhere as he went.

When his face was level with her mound, her pulled her panties out wide and somehow managed to bury his face inside them. She held the material over him, rubbing it against his cheeks as he licked at her pussy, his hands digging into the tops of her stockings.

With one hard tug her pulled away from her and ripped her panties straight off, taking them in his hand to bring to his mouth and suck on the crutch. She, in the meantime, pulled the hood back from her clit and, after dipping her fingers inside what I imagined would be her ultra-hot cunt, smeared the juices over the nub and began to rub.

Fuck, just watching them had me creaming my own panties. I pulled them off quickly, never taking my eyes from the screen. I wished I'd thought to place in a tape. I could have recorded it and watched it whenever I felt like it, but if she ever found out, well, that would be the end of our friendship.

I dipped my fingers into my pussy, loving the feel of my silky juices as they slipped in and out while I continued to watch. Ricky was peeling off his shirt. Man, what a torso. He was rippling with muscles and when he dropped his trousers and jocks and his cock sprung forth, my eyes nearly popped.

He had the biggest cock I've ever seen.

He picked Sarah up and carried her to the bed, throwing her down on it. I was pleased as I could get a better view from this angle. I could hear giggling through the wall but not what they were saying. She lunged for his cock and sucked it deep into her mouth. With both hands on her face he guided her so he was fucking her mouth while she looked up adoringly at him.

No wonder they were always in the bedroom!

Pulling her face away, his cock dropped a fraction, bobbing in front of him, as saliva dripped from the knob. She lay down and opened her legs for him and he dived in between them. She in the meantime was caressing her own breasts, pulling at the nipples, squeezing them so they stood firm and erect.

I grabbed my breast beneath my T-shirt and massaged roughly. I pulled the nipples, wishing desperately that my boyfriend was in here with me. Ricky was eating her as though starved, nuzzling in, poking between her cheeks at her puckered hole.

Then he was inching down her body, kissing her thighs, her claves, her ankles and feet. He lifted one ankle and rested it in the palm of his hand. Undoing the strap he very slowly withdrew her foot from the shoe and rubbed it against his cock. She placed her other foot into his groin and rubbed in hard. He knocked her leg away and slapped her pussy with the flat of the shoe a few times. Her legs fell open wider, as though wanting more.

Man, I never would have thought she'd be into that sort of thing. Slapping my pussy had never entered my mind. He discarded the shoe and looked at her wolfishly, licking his lips and saying something that had her laughing loudly.

Lowering his head, he licked at the stocking, nibbling at her instep. She laughed, pulling her foot back away from him but he hung on tight, taking her toes to his mouth and then sucking them.

I've never seen anyone do that before. I'd heard about stocking fetishes but didn't know anyone who was into it. Sarah certainly must have been because her hand stole down between her thighs and she fiddled with her pussy, clearly loving what he was doing.

Ricky continued to suck on her toes, while her other foot travelled up to his groin. She dug the heel into him as he undid the strapping on this shoe too, allowing it to rub up against him before flipping it from her foot. She knocked his cock with her shoeless foot, trying to grab at it with her toes. He held it there, guiding it all over his shaft and balls. I gasped as I saw his cock grow even bigger.

Fuck, the guy was built like a stallion.

This went on for some time before he finally released her leg, dropping it to the bed. She spread them open, displaying herself for him. His knob was purple, pulsating with blood, as he grabbed it in his palm and guided it to her but instead of fucking her with it, he pulled at one of the stockings, tearing it from the garter and rubbed his cock against it.

Ripping it from her leg, he pulled the stocking over his shaft, covering the knob and bunching it up at his balls. She pulled him closer, guiding it into her opening. He pushed in and his head fell back, his arse cheeks clenched and contracted as he began to fuck her.

Sarah's legs wrapped themselves around his back and she kicked her heels into his arse, urging him on, wanting him to fuck her harder. I watched mesmerized as her fingernails raked down his back, leaving bright red welts wherever they went. She clawed at him, wild with lust as he slammed into her.

I rubbed my clit, wanting desperately to come, pleased when I did that it didn't take as long as usual. I stripped off my clothes, opened my window in the hope of hearing them, and naked, lay back on the bed, my eyes scanning my room for something to use, as I don't have a dildo.

I made a mental note to buy one tomorrow. In the meantime Sarah was now straddling Ricky. He was laying on his back, his magnificent cock high in her pussy. She undid her bra and dropped her massive breasts. He crushed them together, nuzzling into her cleavage as she rode him slowly.

Pulling her forward, so he could nibble at a nipple, made her arse spread, pointing straight at the camera. Her puckered hole winked at me as his hand stole around and he began to inch a finger in slowly. She leaned in further, squashing her breasts against him, grinding her pussy down into his groin until he'd inserted a finger down to the knuckle. From nowhere a dildo appeared and now he inched that into her hole.

I looked at my dressing table and spied a bottle of deodorant. I retrieved it quickly and opened my bedside drawer. I slathered it with lubricating cream that I kept inside for emergencies. Lying on my side, with my knees drawn up, I began to rub it against my own hole. I could still see them and saw that the dildo had nearly disappeared inside her.

She was thrashing about and then, knocking his hand away, she pulled the dildo out and threw it onto across the room. She placed her hands on the wall and began to ride him, slamming down into his groin, wild with desire. Her head thrashed from side to side, her hair flinging about wildly. She was like a crazy woman, fucking him hard until he flipped her over in one go, still impaled on him, and fucked her, pummelling into her until sweat flew in every direction from the two of them.

Now I could hear them through the wall. They were screaming, screaming that they were coming. I wasn't surprised: amazed that anyone could last as long as they had.

Me, I now had the bottle in my pussy, while rubbing my clit madly. It wasn't enough though. I wanted more. Needed a man to make me come like a woman. Finally, Ricky pulled his cock out and sprayed his come all over her breasts. She fell back, her hands caressing it into her flesh, her hair plastered to her face before collapsing against him. He lay there prostrate, his chest rising and falling, his cock flaccid, hanging on the side of his thigh like a huge cobra, still thick, still oozing come.

I picked up the phone beside my bed and rang my boyfriend Frank.

'You still want to do a threesome?' I asked breathlessly.

'What?' he spluttered, obviously disbelieving.

'A threesome. I thought you wanted to do it, baby?' I asked, as throatily and sultry as I could.

'Fuck, yeah,' he laughed. 'You bet.'

'Then get your arse over here. We need to talk and I feel like a fuck,' I giggled.

'I'll be there in a flash,' he said.

I hung up and peered at the screen. Sarah and Ricky were at it again. Fuck, he was horny. I remembered that about a year ago Sarah had asked me if I'd ever be interested in a threesome and at the time I'd said no. Well, now that I've seen her in action, it was time to take her up on it. And with any luck we'd end up having a foursome, with that stallion of hers, Ricky.

I could hardly wait for Frank. My pussy was tingling with anticipation and as soon as he walked in my bedroom door and saw me naked on the bed we were at it like two dogs on heat.

I'll be sure to let you know how it all pans out.

An Unknown Force
by Eva Hore

It was dark and deadly quiet in the little cabin that I'd rented for the weekend. Apart from the rustling of leaves, as the wind ripped them from their branches to scatter over the porch, and the trickling of water as it gently cascaded over rocks that joined into the creek, it was exactly what I'd wanted. Peace and tranquillity, no phones, no neighbours, nothing to do but sit and relax. I was coming to terms with the break-up of my marriage.

Bone tired, I closed the door behind me and headed out to explore. The lounge had an open fire and a comfortable suite, the kitchen looked quite trendy with all modern appliances and the bathroom was gleaming, the scented towels thick and luxurious, the spa inviting.

The bedroom was quaint compared to the rest of the cabin, decked out in old fashion furniture, a four poster bed with mosquito netting draped over fluffed up pillows and duvet gave it a mystical feel and I wondered who else had slept in this bed and why.

'Probably someone on their honeymoon,' I muttered to myself as I checked the bed linen was fresh.

Packing away the few things I'd brought with me I set about lighting the fire in the hearth and some candles. I was too tired to enjoy the spa, so donned my nightie and opened a bottle of wine.

I lay back to enjoy the isolation and ponder my future. The wind whistled and a distant boom of thunder promised rain was on its way. I was onto my third glass and had just reached over to pick it up when an icy chill ran down my spine and the temperature in the room dropped.

Frightened and alarmed, I quickly scanned the room. Nothing! I slipped out of bed checking the doors and windows. They were all locked. A few splats of heavy rain hit the old tin roof, probably what caused the temperature to drop. Shrugging off my nervousness I settled back into bed, snuggling in further and, as I did, the candles began to flicker, casting long shadows across the walls, almost going out before they glowed again.

I knew I'd locked the windows and the doors were definitely secured, so why would the candles be flickering? There wasn't a draft anywhere. That uneasiness returned and I tried hard to fight down a panic attack.

A weight pressing down on the duvet frightening me. I gasped and half-screamed out, pulling the duvet right up to my chin as though to ward it off. It lifted but I had the distinct impression it settled at the foot of the bed. It happened so quickly I wasn't sure if I'd imagined it or not. I reached over and downed my drink, laughing nervously.

I don't usually sleep with candles lit but now I was too scared to blow them out. Burrowing back down, I closed my eyes and unexpectedly the duvet began to levitate. I yanked it back, tucking it around me and closed my eyes tightly. I didn't want to see anything. I was so frightened. Something tugged, I pulled back.

It kept tugging, yanking furiously. It would let go, then all of a sudden it would stop. I'd relax my grip slightly and then it would again try to wrench it from me. I don't know how long this went on, I lost track of time. It was playing with me, that was obvious. Finally, fear gave way to curiosity and I allowed the duvet to be torn from me and watched it thrown into a corner of the room.

I lay there breathing hard. My eyes searching every inch of the room for something, some sort of vision, a being, a hint of what was in this room with me. The word poltergeist, and that horror movie from years ago, the one with the girl whose head spun around, filled my mind.

Seconds ticked by, then minutes. I was beginning to think it had gone. I wondered what it was thinking, what it wanted from me and was beginning to think it had gone and went to sit up, but I was pushed back, not by fingers but by a cold puff of air.

Now my nightie was being inched up my thigh, very slowly, so slowly that my eyes were riveted to it, trying to see how this was possible. An icy trail ran over my flesh, causing goosebumps to form over my skin wherever it touched. I held my breath as it circled my breasts. I hadn't realised I was holding my breath and suddenly, as two cold hands grabbed at me, I screamed. Something descended over my lips, forcing my mouth to open while a cold tongue snaked in and slithered inside.

I was breathing hard, frightened yet exhilarated. This was the most incredible sensation. I tried to relax as the hands roamed over my body leaving goosebumps wherever they went.

A tugging at my ankles as it tried to pull my legs apart had me struggling at first but it was too determined, so in the end I allowed it all to happen. Hands were roaming over my pubic hair, then down over my slit. I shuddered with longing as my flaps were pulled apart and icy fingers explored me.

I licked my lips enjoying the icy touch. My own hands went to my breasts and I massaged them as I squirmed on the bed but then they were slapped away, pulled up and tied

133

with something to the bed head. I tugged, trying to free myself, frightened at being in this vulnerable position.

There was movement between my thighs and something hard probed my lips.

I peered out of the slits in my eyes wanting to see this thing, this being that was ravishing my body, but nothing was there. I opened my legs wider and thought I heard a chuckle as fingers stretched my lips wide open.

I wiggled deeper into the bed, titillated, no longer frightened, now enjoying this erotic encounter. A cock or something like one was inching its way inside me. I opened my eyes wide, searching the room for some indication to what this thing was. I could see nothing but felt everything.

I gasped with desire when my nightie was ripped from my body as hands roamed all over me while something pushed and shoved its way inside my hot pussy. I thrust back up into it, loving it, moaning with pleasure as a mouth descended cruelly upon me and icy lips covered my face.

Now I was bucking back into it, my arms straining while my legs encircled nothing but were able to hold up against this invisible force. It was fucking amazing. It slammed into me over and over and I came and came, nearly delirious with pleasure and then, just as quick as it came, it released me and disappeared.

It left me alone and just vanished. I lay there staring up at the ceiling hoping it would come back, but it didn't. Pulling the duvet over my battered body I eventually fell into a restless sleep.

The next morning I woke tired and exhausted. My body displaying all the signs of a good fucking. I ran the bath and eased my sore and aching body into the warm scented water. I was thrilled when soapy hands covered me, caressing, washing and exploring my body. I lay back, opened my legs to enjoy the best bath I've had in years.

Rising, a towel enveloped me and busily began to dry me. The fear from last night left me and inquisitiveness and eagerness took over. Wanting desperately to see this thing that entered me last night I searched my handbag and came up with a condom.

I jumped back onto the bed, ripped open the package and left it lying on the pillow. It lifted into the air, stretched it open and rolled it down the biggest shaft I've ever seen. This cock was massive. No it was bigger than that, bigger than John Holmes, bigger than anything I've ever seen.

And all I could see was the cock.

My eyes opened wide as it inched itself inside me.

'Oh yeah,' I breathed, as he began to fuck me rhythmically.

Hands slapped at my thighs as I reached out and pulled him to me. I lifted my legs, encircling his waist as he fucked me mercilessly. Then he rolled me over, pulled me up by the hips so I was in the doggy position and slammed straight back into my pussy.

It was fucking awesome.

Desperate to please this apparition I pushed him away from me and lunged towards his cock. Trying hard I managed to swallow half of him, he was so huge that I honestly thought my mouth would split as I began to suck him off.

I groped around and felt his icy balls. Cupping them in my hand I squeezed gently at first and then a bit harder. He seemed to like that. His hands held my head as he pumped himself into my mouth.

I felt him stiffen and then I was gagging as he thrust himself deep into my mouth. Finally he withdrew this monstrous cock and I could see by the end of the condom that he must have shot gallons of semen in there as the condom was stretched a further four inches. I pulled it off him and threw it on the floor.

135

Suddenly my bag was opened and condoms were being ripped out of their packets. Dozens of cocks appeared around me and as hands held my legs and arms open I was fucked continually in every position imaginable.

I've never in my life experienced anything that could compare to this. Every orifice was sucked, fucked and licked.

My favourite was sitting astride one, his cock high in my pussy, while another ravished my hole. Then another was ramming a cock in my mouth while hands pinched and pulled at my nipples. I've never come so much in my life and let's face it, it was certainly the safest sex I've ever had.

No STD's from these guys I can tell you.

I spent three days there, being fucked in every position imaginable and only God knows by who. I left exhausted but sated and promised them I'd be back soon, very soon.

Devils And Angels
by Fransiska Sherwood

'Nice machine.' I finger the chrome fender, my head cocked saucily to one side.

Its owner stares, unable to believe such audacity.

He's one of those ageing Easy Rider types – about fifty, at a guess. The bike's a vintage Harley.

'Go play someplace else, little girl,' he growls in a voice that's deep and gravelly, and smacks of wind, weather, axle grease and sex.

'Only trying to be friendly,' I reply.

'I don't need any friends.' He turns his back on me with a frown.

'Hmm.' I smile to myself. This isn't going to be as simple as I thought. But he's the only way I can see of getting away from here right now.

He swaggers off to pay for his tank-full, the leather tassels that hang off him at every seam swaying like a cat-o'-nine-tails as he goes. Like the bike, the gear's all authentic – right down to the pot helmet and spurs on his boots.

I wait to see if anyone else pulls up at the pumps. They don't. It's a sleepy little place. The kind of town you pass through on your way to somewhere better. A place that bores me rigid.

I watch the grumpy old sod drink a coffee inside before he returns. An ambling bear – more grizzly than teddy – but there's something cuddly about him, nevertheless.

'You still here?'

'Looks like it, doesn't it?'

His whiskers twitch. A sweeping moustache of grey that cascades over his mouth, concealing an involuntary smirk.

'Trying to cadge a ride?'

I give my sweetest smile, and throw back my head. 'Thanks. I'd love to.'

He scowls, flicks his ponytail aside and reties his neckerchief. 'Ever ridden anything like this before?'

If he only knew what kind of guys I've been for rides with.

'Reckon I'm just out of nappies, do you?' For a last-ditch attempt to win him over, it maybe wasn't the best of lines.

He begins to strap on his helmet, eyeing me as he does so. There's a definite spark of interest in that look. Blonde might just be his type. But then he swings his leg over the saddle and my heart sinks. I guess you can't wind everybody round your little finger.

He pulls on a pair of gloves with flared cuffs. And then, to my amazement, retrieves a helmet from one of the black leather saddlebags. He tosses it to me. I catch it and flash him a grin. One he returns with a hint of annoyance.

He watches as I shake back my hair and put on the helmet.

Maybe he's not such a lone wolf as he likes to make out. And not so bad, either. If you're into raw hide and whiskers. As he grips the handlebars, arms outstretched, I'm reminded of Dennis Hopper and Peter Fonda, decades earlier. Cult figures to a whole generation. The very symbols of freedom.

I climb onto the seat behind him.

'Wanna go any place particular?' he asks over his shoulder.

'Just out into the country.'

Anywhere away from here and its stifling, middle-class tedium.

I zip up my red leather jacket, thanking the skies above there was an autumn chill in the air today and I'm wearing stiletto ankle boots and jeans, not something flimsy. All designer labels, deliberately worn cheap.

He kick-starts the engine and gives it some throttle, playing with the throaty roar a few times before letting it carry us away.

I slip my hands round his hips and huddle close to him, the biting tang of leather stinging my nostrils and transporting me to a forgotten land of road movies and westerns. Even if these weekend Hell's Angels often turn out to be doctors or lawyers.

When we get out into the open he really lets the machine rip, tearing up the tarmac with a deafening rumble.

His earlier question was valid – riding a Harley is like nothing I've ever experienced. It's as if a swarm of hornets are trapped beneath my seat, getting angrier and angrier the faster we go. A buzzing underneath me that soon starts to invade my flesh; first of all a mere tingling in my bottom that grows to a hum and works itself up through my sex, threatening to drive me insane.

I curse the responsiveness of my body. I can do without this just now. Although at other times I crave the pangs of want that shoot through me.

I push myself hard onto the saddle, close up against his pelvis. 'I've got to stop. My bum's gone numb,' I shout into his ear. Although numbness is the last sensation I'm experiencing right now.

He glances back at me and I note the tell-tale, crow's-foot creases of a smile.

139

We cruise down an allée lined with old chestnuts, their leafy canopy making a green tunnel of the road. My flesh is now purring along with the engine.

At the next opportunity we pull into a field gateway, spraying pebbles into the grass. I swing my leg over the saddle with relief, wondering just how much of this very particular tickling I could have withstood before I keeled off the bike.

'Backside need a pummelling, does it?' he asks as we take off our helmets. Above the neckerchief, still pulled up over his nose, his eyes twinkle at me, crinkled at the corners by a stealthy grin I can't see. He may have seemed like a surly old codger at first, but he's got a wicked streak, if I can trust my intuition.

I flutter my eyelashes. 'Ooh, that would be nice!'

Still wearing the gloves, he flexes his fingers and wiggles them a bit. But from the sudden serious look on his face I realise he's not clowning. And we both know my exclamation of mock pleasure wasn't purely pretend.

I look into his eyes. Hazel eyes that I now notice are speckled with flecks of yellow. Like some animal's. An animal I could befriend, or something dangerous?

I hesitate for a moment, wondering if this is wise, but knowing that I'm a sucker for an older man and any kind of adventure. Then I turn and offer him my bottom, enticingly neat in the tight jeans.

He kneels down behind me, and a frisson of excitement ripples through me. I could be in for something special.

Clad in the leather gloves, he starts to knead the cheeks of my bottom, working the flesh with expert hands, moulding it with firm, practised movements, a few exploratory strokes coming excruciatingly close to the aching lips of my sex.

'That hard enough for you?'

'Just right.' And it's doing things to me worse than those induced by the bike.

I hear him give a throaty hum in return, before he continues the treatment. Is he enjoying this as much as I am?

Yet after a while this pleasure no longer does enough for me. I'm craving something more.

'Let's pretend I've been a naughty girl, and it's your job to deliver my punishment,' I say.

I look to see if his whiskers twitch. They do, and the corners of his eyes crease up, too. Much to my satisfaction.

'If I'm to know how severe the punishment is to be, I need to know what the crime was.'

I begin to wonder if he is indeed a lawyer. But it really doesn't matter if he's going to take me up on the game.

'I'm a repeat offender – all the wrong kind of boyfriends. And I don't regret a thing. I'm in need of some hard disciplining, so don't be too lenient.'

He gives his throaty laugh. 'I'd say you deserve a good leathering.'

I smile. Just the verdict I was hoping for.

He takes off the gloves and strikes me on the bottom.

'Too soft,' I say, 'I can hardly feel a thing through my jeans.'

'We can soon put that right – if you really want to.'

Do I really want to? You bet I do.

I undo the zip to my jeans and pull them down, receiving a smack on one cheek the moment it peeks from beneath my string tanga.

But this spank was only a playful one. A mere foretaste of what's to come. A little starter to test my willingness.

'Harder!' I say.

And harder I get. My skin sings as if it's just been stung. And he does it again and again, until my flesh is just one big, red-hot tingle.

'Like that, do you?'

'Oh, yes,' I moan.

'Then you really are a very naughty girl.'

It's not long before a leather finger strays between the folds of my sex and the string of lace. I don't protest – quite the contrary – so he starts to rub and caress me, then seeks out the nub of my clitoris and winds little circles round it, while the other hand saucily clasps the cheek of my bottom.

Then, without warning, he pushes his way into me, his finger like a leather cock massaging my inner walls. I gasp with surprise and delight.

Soon spasms are shooting through my cervix more urgently than ever before. Pulsating contractions he can surely feel.

'Punishment fit the crime?'

'Oh yes.'

A tingling wave of pleasure now floods my body, more furious than that released by the angry swarm of hornets under my seat. A climax so violent and sudden it leaves me reeling in its wake.

Then he strikes my cheek with one of the gloves again. Pain that only heightens my enjoyment. The whole of my body is one aching mass. I don't know how much more of it I can take, but I want it to continue, fast and frantic, for ever.

And he doesn't let up until every fibre in me is quaking.

'Had enough now?'

He gives a few final thrusts with his finger as I gasp and moan, my body helpless with ecstasy. I couldn't hang on to the bike now if I tried.

Then, abruptly, he pulls his finger out and rolls me onto my side. I collapse onto the ground, my body awash with the ebbing spasms of pleasure still rippling through me.

'Is this game reciprocal?' he asks after a moment or two.

My eyes sweep over the criss-cross laces at his flies. There's a definite bump in his leather trousers. A wicked grin creeps across my face as I start to imagine all the things still in store for me. I knew my prospects were exciting the moment I set eyes on that bike.

In answer I ease my clingy, black, jersey top over my head and drop it on the floor beside me. A low whistle of appreciation tells me he likes what he sees.

'You know, you look like butter wouldn't melt in your mouth, but really you're as guilty as sin.' The yellow flecks in his eyes flicker like sparks.

He pinches open the hooks to my bra and pulls the lacy padding from me. The straps slip from my shoulders and stroke my skin the way I'm yearning for him to do. All over. Every inch of me.

He pulls on the tasselled gloves and begins to trace little circles round my nipples with one of the fingers. The leather's cool and coarse. Not a soft, silky caress. More the serrated tongue of a whip strap. And I love it.

The palms of his gloved hands then close over my breasts, gently kneading, like they did to my bottom.

How I wish he'd do that again.

Soon I'm aching once more with pent-up desire. I begin to fiddle with his lace-up flies. I really dig this gear: all the tassels, its smell. Then, when I can't take any more of the kneading (and waiting), I ease open the thongs, prising the criss-cross strips of leather wider apart until the snow white material of his underpants becomes visible.

For a moment or two I wonder whether to wriggle the leather trousers down over his hips and slip him out of his snowy briefs, or whether this biker's uniform doesn't offer more enticing possibilities. Far beyond those permitted by normal clothing.

I don't deliberate for long. Tantalised by still unimagined prospects, I reach between the laces and feel

143

my way inside the pouch of his Y-fronts where his cock snuggles. For a few moments I fondle its already rigid shaft, then carefully extricate it from the confines of the fabric. I pull the laces tight again, so the trousers once more sit close at his hips, his cocking protruding from the crotch.

I take it in my hands. Then my lips close round the glistening skin and I let my tongue play with its sensitive end, wallowing in the smell of leather that surrounds him and seems to be his own.

When I come up, there's a devilish grin on his face.

If he wants, this is only the beginning. And when we've finished, after all I've got in mind, I'll deserve a good spanking.

Layla Raises Cane
by Virginia Beech

I lie in the darkness of my bedroom, trying to sleep, but unable to relax enough to drift off. I think of the strange twists in my life before my career as a front page supermodel and dominatrix took off.

Meeting up with Harry was one of the stranger episodes. It was to change my hitherto vanilla lifestyle and set me on the road as an enthusiastic dominatrix. At the time I was the Third Floor fashion model at an exclusive Knightsbridge department store near Sloane Street in London's West End. It was a spring-board job modelling the store's Womenswear. It kept me, paying my half of the rent for the basement pad I shared with Hyacinth around the corner in Lowndes Square until we got ourselves a top agent and hit it big on the catwalks. On that chilly day in February, Hyacinth was away on a photo shoot and I was on my way out of the store after a long day modelling outfits from the Spring collection. Passing through 'Lingerie', on my way to the elevator, I noticed this tall, distinguished-looking gentleman sporting a Gieves blazer and Household Cavalry tie. He was standing at the boutique panty bar, presumably buying something sexy for a lady friend. That's a lucky girl who has him put them on her and then take them off again, I thought idly. I heard him ask the sales assistant whether she had something in oyster satin, trimmed with lace. Classy tastes too, I thought.

While she was busy dealing with his request, I saw him snaffle a pair of lace-trimmed silk knickers from a pile on the counter and hurriedly stuff them into his blazer pocket. I stopped and pretended to look at some retro-seamed stockings at the next counter. He bought and paid for the knickers the assistant showed him with plastic and, thinking that nobody had noticed his 'Buy One – Get One Free' gambit, he made his way to the lift.

I followed him, intending to point him out to the store detective at the entrance. But then I had a much better idea. I shadowed him out of the store into Knightsbridge and as soon as he was out on the street, I was right behind his sorry ass... his ass was mine! He was a good-looking, sexy bastard, with fair hair, beautiful blue/grey eyes, and was doubtless a 'high goal' demon on the polo field at Windsor. I stepped up to his side, flashed the store ID tag on the inside of my jacket, and said, 'Sir, you will have to come me. I saw you steal the knickers you have in your blazer pocket!'

He was thoroughly demoralised at that and looked at me so pathetically that I was almost sorry for being the unfeeling bitch I am! He said quietly and calmly, 'Isn't there something we can work out about this? I am a Guards officer and if this gets out I'll be cashiered.'

'You should have thought of that when you decided to rip off our store! We know your name from your credit card so just come quietly with me, please!'

I took him by the arm and before he had time to think I had whisked him round the corner into Lowndes Square and down the steps to my basement flat. He looked so bleak and pathetic, and I was giggling inside. He was obviously a closet transvestite who just loved the sensual feel of fine fabrics next to his skin – and, hell, I understood that!

I guided him into my pad, closed the door, locked it and turned to him with a grin of satisfaction. He was appraising me, with his blue eyes twinkling now. Then I was all over him.

He was laughing with relief and looking at me with admiration and growing lust!

'That was a cruel way to make my acquaintance!'

'I haven't made your acquaintance yet, but, in just a few moments, I'm going to!' I said, as I gave his lip a playful nip. He laughed out loud then and kissed my mouth like he knew what the fuck he was doing! I liked it! I knew I would, though.

I led the way to my bedroom, peeling off my coat as I went. He followed me in and I turned to face him. I was up real close and personal, breathing in the heady fragrance of his cologne as I loosened his Guards tie and eased him out of his jacket.

'You nearly gave me a heart attack on the street in front of the store! What made you think of pretending to be a store detective like that, you little bitch!'

'I had a 'Go to Hell' attitude overtake me when I saw you stealing these knickers,' I replied, jerking them out of his blazer pocket and dangling them enticingly beneath his nose.

'I was going to scare the pants off you for the fun of it, then I saw how edibly handsome you are and decided to play you and reel you in for my pleasure instead. Now, strip and do exactly as I tell you! Let's see what you look like in this pretty pair of knickers that you stole.'

I enjoyed the view as he stripped off his clothes. He was in marvellous shape and I could see by his ramrod military erection, which rose stiffly to attention under my appreciative gaze, that I was going to have a wonderful night instead of eating alone. I looked at this Adonis, whose name I didn't know and thought that he was more shocked

147

now than when I tricked him into coming here with me. He put on the sheer black silky panties with lace trim that barely covered his throbbing manhood and turned toward me. I reached for the silky bulge of his rock hard cock and stroked it through the straining fabric. I could feel his cock quiver as I ran my lacquered nail up and down its heated shaft. He bent to kiss my mouth, giving me his tongue to suck. And I sucked it! God, did I suck it!

I kicked off my Jimmy Choo heels, unzipped my vintage fashion skirt and let it slither to the floor. 'Undress me!' I commanded huskily. 'Undress me slowly!'

He started on the buttons of my blouse, kissing me between each opened button, breathing in the bloom of my body fragrance as he progressed, until he could ease it off my shoulders. Letting it drop to the floor, he ran his hands lingeringly down over the contours of my satin slip, caressing the curves of my breasts, hips and buttocks through the sensual material before easing it off my shoulders to pull it down, his hands brushing my nipples through my lace bra as they passed. He knelt and dragged the slip over my hips and tummy and then his hands were lingering on my inner thighs and he was lowering my knickers an inch at a time until he had fully exposed my pussy to his hungry gaze.

I was getting really hot from his delicate touch on my skin and the way that this scene was unfolding. I knew that my cunt was wet and I was anticipating the coming events with great relish as he nuzzled his face against the landing strip of my Brazilian. I felt his tongue flick all too briefly at my cunt lips before he rose, took me into his arms and kissed me a crushing kiss filled with terrible need.

I knew it had been a while for this handsome stranger with a penchant for naughty knickers. He had his hands on my breasts now, almost frantic with desire for me and I wanted to keep him that way, self-serving bitch that I am!

I caressed his hot meat some more beneath the straining tautness of those becomingly feminine knickers and felt the pre-cum drops through the thin fabric. I delved into the silk and slowly lifted his hard cock and balls out from their tight prison. He was quite ready to melt in my hand. I would have him melt in my mouth later! He was soooooooooooo near to exploding! He had that glazed look that foretold his approaching ecstasy.

I looked into those half-closed eyes and said sternly, 'Not yet, my sexy slave! You come when I tell you, and not a second before!' I gave his rampant cock a disciplinary slap. 'This is *my* game and you play by *my* rules. It's 'Ladies First' in *my* household. Your mistress decides when and how she wants her cumcream delivered. Is that understood?'

He looked at me hungrily but, with his balls firmly clasped in my hot little hand, he was in no position to argue. He nodded and breathed a rasping, 'Yes!'

With that I put his hand on my pussy. 'Find your mistress's priceless pearl!'

His finger parted my pussy lips, found my clit and began to rub it, massaging it into excited hardness. My legs began to quiver and I was almost riding his finger now. He was making me feel really good. He frigged me harder as my clit stiffened and I moaned to his rhythmic movement. I wanted to call out his name, but I didn't know what the fuck it was! Right then 'Slave' came to mind.

'Deeper now, Slave!' I panted. 'Harder! Faster!'

He began to finger fuck my hot hole, kissing my neck and then sucking and nibbling at my excitedly erect nipples. My legs were giving way and I backed onto the bed before I collapsed, pulling him down on top of me.

'Keep frigging and suck my tits!' I managed to gasp.

'Yes! Yes! You're on it!' My pantie thief had me on fire now; ready to come as he kept up the pace, frigging my clit with his thumb and finger-fucking my cunt with his other fingers. I felt my climax rising deep within my belly. I arched my body, clawing his back with my nails as the ecstasy overtook me. I was coming in racking waves that pounded on the shores of my body.

I took his tongue, sucking hard and moaning as each quivering wave pulsed through me. Then, as the dying waves of ecstasy ebbed from the beach of my body, came the moment of serene euphoria; the blissful calm after the storm. He held me close, whispering adoring filth in my ear. And I loved every fucking word!

I moved him off me and I looked at his precious penis. It stood so patiently at attention, ready to perform its duty at my command. I wrapped my fingers possessively around its warm hardness.

'You ready for Mistress's hot juicy cunt?' I said, leaning close to inspect its finer attributes and speaking directly to it. I shook it up and down as if it was saying 'Yes, Mistress!' What a magnificent beast I was about to tame! 'A cock in the hand is worth two in the bush,' as dear Mummy would always say after one too many gins!

I looked it in the eye. 'I have a really deep desire for you. And it looks like you've got a good head for business,' I murmured, caressing the throbbing blood-engorged glans appreciatively, 'I am offering you entry to "The Gates of Heaven", but your owner must storm those gates and fuck me like he's never fucked before! And he must tell me he worships me and talk dirty to me, because I just love that when I've got a big hard cock like you inside me.'

Fancy panties looked at me. 'Shut up, my proud filly and lie back! I shall ride you to the gallop!' He opened my legs and put them back to gaze at my Venus mound's expensive Brazilian topiary. Then he aimed his lance and thrust. I grunted as it glided slickly into the inviting wetness of my tight hole. Its hot girth filled me. He began fucking me slowly, thrusting harder, deeper with each stroke, screwing me to the bed. I was loving it so much, rising up to meet each powerful thrust, my legs wrapped around him, urging him ever deeper inside my belly.

I was in a wild, fucking frenzy and hardly conscious of anything but our heated bodies and the exquisite slippery friction between us as he spurred me onward to the gallop. He was straining, grunting and moaning in his headlong, sweat-bathed ecstasy.

I pounded on his back with my fists, clawed him in my delirium. 'God, yes! I love it, fuck me, baby! I want it! I want it all! Give it to me! Love me! Make me come, darling! Fuck me! Fuck me! Fuck me!' I screamed in a rictus of orgasmic ecstasy.

And he FUCKED ME! God, I had never been so fucked in my life! He was to die for and I knew right there and then, that this was the lover of my dreams! I knew I would never be fucked this royally again. We came at the same instant; me screaming and kissing his mouth and sucking his tongue and he hammering me as he spurted his hot love cream into my guts, his balls slapping my ass.

Finally he was spent and collapsed on top of me. We lay there in mutual euphoric stupor, his head upon my shoulder, his breast heaving from his headlong charge into my breach.

I opened my eyes and looked at the sweet face I reckoned I now owned. 'Who the hell are you? Where have you been all my life?'

He rolled off of me to lie beside me, slipped my head onto his strong arm and looked adoringly into my eyes.

'Hello, Precious Pussy! I'm Harry, and I'm now your devoted slave!'

I looked searchingly into the blue of his beautiful eyes and knew that this was the beginning of a very long affair; a journey to the furthest reaches of sensual discovery, as I moulded this superb rider to my exotic whims. But there was just one little problem that I needed to address first!

'Harry, darling, you have been a bad bad boy, nicking naughty knickers! What if someone else had seen you? You would now be at Knightsbridge police station having your fingerprints taken and making a statement before they called your C.O. at Knightsbridge Barracks. Your Mistress is going to teach you a memorable lesson, so you are never tempted to pinch panties again. In future, when you lust for lingerie to clothe your handsome body, you will call me and I shall be right here to dress you in the silks and satins you so lust after. And after I've dressed you as my adoring slut and you have donned my frilly knickers, I shall take them down and whip that lovely ass of yours until you come! How does that sound? Do we have a deal, darling?'

I felt a quiver of excitement course through Harry's body at the thought of my domination. I was quivering at the thought too!

'Now, get off my bed. I haven't finished with you yet!'

I patted that muscled rump of his. 'Put those black silk knickers back on, sweetcheeks, and then get into my satin slip and lace-top thigh-highs. I want to see what a rampant shemale looks like when dressed to please her mistress!'

Shock, surprise and delight passed in rapid succession over Harry's face as my commands registered with him. He began to dress silently, donning my fine lingerie with evident delight. He really looked quite fetching dressed like that. He turned to admire himself in my full-length mirror, running his hands down over his satin-clad body. I saw a nascent bulge manifest itself beneath the satin folds of my borrowed slip as his dormant cock returned to life in the excitement of the occasion. I doubt if this was the first time Harry had admired himself in such finery. Now, at last, he had an appreciative and supportive mistress to share his secret feminine fantasies.

It was time for slave to submit to mistress and accept a first painful lesson in obedience. I donned my black kimono and led him by the hand to the kitchen and stood him in front of the heavy pine table.

'Bend over the table and put your arms out in front of you! I am going to cane you. It will be your first lesson in obedience to my will and a reminder never to steal naughty knickers again.'

I picked up a whippy length of rattan which I had bought at the Saturday Pimlico Farmers' Market to support my potted tomato plant.

A look of disbelief came over Harry's face as my words sank home. But, dressed like that, he was in no position to quibble over mistress's decision. I tapped the table with my improvised cane and motioned to him to position himself as ordered.

I found the sight of his humiliating position bent over the table most pleasing. I felt a wetness between my legs at the exciting prospect of caning an inviting ass for the very first time. It would be a profane waste for this cane to prop up a humble tomato plant after its sacred use in the first bonding of a Domina and her slave.

The silken fabric of Harry's purloined panties stretched tightly over the spheres I was about to whip, clinging like a second skin to their firm roundness.

I arranged the satin folds of the slip over his back and slid my hand into the warmth of Harry's knickers, lowering the clinging garment to expose the cheeks I was about to chastise. The material rustled sensuously as it slithered down his stockinged thighs.

'Open your legs wide! Stretch those knickers taut between your knees! I must be able to see your dangling jewels for your ass to be properly positioned for my caning.'

I was beginning to enjoy this dominatrix power bit as I

153

created our private punishment ritual. Harry was docile and silent in his acceptance and trust in my domination of his body. I felt between his open legs, fondling his dangling balls and teasingly caressing his dormant cock. I hoped a well striped ass would excite it to new vitality for our post-punishment pleasure. The thought titillated me and, presumably, Harry. His cock swelled sweetly to my touch. Such punishment ritual could become mutually addictive.

Harry's ass cheeks were now perfectly framed between slip, stockings and knickers for my visual delight. I reached for my digital camera and recorded this unique moment in our budding relationship.

I gripped the cane firmly and whipped through the air to get the feel of it. I stood back and took a deep breath. My heart was pounding at what I was about to do. I raised my arm.

Crack!

'We shall count each stroke together, Harry. One! That has left a most pleasing red weal across your tender cheeks. It shall be my marker for the rest.'

Crack!

'Two! I've left a second scarlet line across your butt, just above the first. Do you feel its fiery imprint, Harry, my love? Your bottom is twitching most erotically to the painful rhythm of my cane. I am getting quite turned on by our scene. Are you?'

Crack!

'Three! That one really hurt, didn't it! Was it like this when you were caned at Eton? But you weren't wearing my sexy lingerie then, were you! So I don't suppose it was such a turn-on for you and your caner!'

Three parallel lines of stinging red had cut across those handsome cheeks, bringing a grunt from Harry as he counted each stroke. I paused to run my hand lovingly over the red welts I had raised, feeling their warmth, enjoying the squirming of his bottom cheeks to my tender touch which he obviously found as sensually arousing as I did.

'Your striped cheeks look very beautiful in their red-lined pain. We must do this more often. Perhaps we can buy you some fine lace-trimmed stockings and a nice suspender belt of your own... and some high heels for you to wear when I cane you. Would you like that, Harry?'

Harry gave what I took to be an approving grunt at my inspired suggestion.

I decided to apply a fourth and last stroke of my cane; lower down on the tender crease between bottom and thigh. Since becoming an accomplished dominatrix with an adoring Harry seeking to cater to my every whim, I have learned that this is what Dominas call the 'Sweet Spot' because it is the most tender and erogenous spot on a bared bottom, engendering the most lustful desire for post-punishment play.

Crack!

'Four! Aaaagh!' Harry cried. He shot upright, clutching his tortured rump to protect it from further damage. I was really hot for more sex now and I could feel a wetness in my cunt that needed urgent attention from cock or tongue. The pain had been pleasure for Harry, judging from the massive erection he now sported after such a ritual punishment scene.

I put the cane down on the table and led Harry by his rampant cock to the sitting room couch. I sat myself down, opened my kimono and spread my legs wide, splaying my conch lips open with my fingers to present my clit for his immediate attention.

'Kneel before me my darling slut stud and suck me!'

I pulled his head toward me and thrust his hot face to my pussy.

'Suck, Harry! Suck my pearl! I'm your mistress now! Take me to Domina paradise!'

I was panting with desire as my climax rose, peaked and overflowed. I clutched Harry's head, holding it to my cunt, pressing his slurping tongue to my Pleasure Fountain and came in a flood-tide of quivering waves that reached to every tingling nerve in my body.

Harry drank deep at the Pleasure Fountain of my fragrantly flowing love-juices and then abruptly stood. His cock, free of any restraining knickers, stood hot and hard ready for mistress; its succulent mushroom head throbbing enticingly before my hungry eyes.

I love to suck a hot cock full of cream, and this was a particularly luscious lollypop that was bobbing before my lips.

'Since you have been such a good submissive to my first ever caning, I shall allow you to face fuck me while I fondle and milk your warm jewels of their precious nectar. But, next time, I shall have you better dressed for the occasion in a proper Slutmaid's uniform. And when you're dressed I shall collar you. Your Slutname shall be Harriet and you will belong to me, your mistress. Do you accept my bargain?'

The look on Harry's face told me all I needed to know. I took that delicious cock in my mouth and began to suck. I had discovered a new lifestyle and I had a willing slave to share it with me!

Holding Out For A Hero
by Elizabeth Coldwell

I was about to leave the party when I spotted him. I've always hated fancy-dress dos. Blame it on too many weekends at university being persuaded to go to parties where the dress code was togas made from bed sheets, or had themes like 'come as you were when the ship went down', which always seemed to be dreamed up in the hope that the hottest babe in the hall of residence would turn up in a skimpy nightie.

But Gillian had told me that I needed to get out and meet more men, and her boss's fortieth birthday bash would be an ideal opportunity.

Of course, she had bumped into Barry from accounts, who was the reason she had accepted the invitation on our behalf, within ten minutes of arriving; the two of them had disappeared to the kitchen together, leaving me to stand by the punch bowl and wonder how much longer I had to leave it before I could slip away without looking like Belinda No-mates.

'Come as your hero,' the invitation had read. For the male guests, that was someone they had particularly admired when they were 15, judging by the outfits on display. Two Indiana Joneses, one of whom was Tony, the party's host, and three different incarnations of Doctor

157

Who. In addition there was Laurel and Hardy, a bloke in full Chelsea kit and someone sporting a boiler suit and ski mask who could either have been Hannibal Lecter or a particularly sadistic plumber; no one who even inspired me to go over and chat, let alone pushed my erotic buttons.

So when I saw him strut over to help himself to a plastic cup of the vodka-laden punch, I thought he had been sent especially to treat me. Very few people could do justice to the costume he had chosen, but on him it looked magnificent. He was wearing very little more than a red cloak and a tight-fitting pair of leather-look shorts. His bare arms and torso were almost indecently muscular, his tousled, dirty-blond hair fell to his shoulders and I could happily have spent all evening licking his broad thighs.

The fact he was carrying an obviously plastic sword did little to damage the illusion that he was a proud Spartan warrior, and, even if it had, I could hardly complain. My own costume, cobbled together from what was lying around at the bottom of my wardrobe, consisted of a khaki-coloured T-shirt, black shorts and hiking boots designed to give me a passing resemblance to Lara Croft. I had scraped my hair back in a ponytail, letting a couple of strands fall over my eyes, and I had a water pistol strapped to my thigh. So, if nothing else, I had the fake weaponry as an opening conversational gambit – if only I could stop weaving dirty little fantasies in my head for long enough to say hello to him.

In my mind, I was already stripped to the waist and on my knees before him, hands secured behind me, while he lazily stroked his cock and looked down on me, smiling cruelly. In moments, that cock would be in my mouth, and I would be made to suck him till he came. It would taste good, salty and male, and though I would display a measure of reluctance to be used by him in this way, in reality I would be loving every minute of it.

158

The realisation that he had noticed me staring snapped me out of my pleasantly filthy daydream, and I smiled sheepishly at him. 'Sorry,' I said, 'I was just admiring your – er – outfit. I'm Lisa, by the way.'

'Darren.' I thought he was going to offer me his hand to shake. Instead, he ran it through his hair in a gesture which sent a spasm of lust through me. 'Yeah, well, you've got to look up to people who took such good care of themselves, haven't you?'

That wasn't exactly the point of being a Spartan, I thought, but I would let it go. 'You must have to put in a lot of work to end up with a body like that?'

'Tell me about it,' he said. 'I do four sessions at the gym a week. Mostly free weights, forty reps on each, then ten miles on the treadmill. I mean, I don't want to look too bulky, but I do like to have defined abs.' Defined? They practically screamed, 'Look at me, touch me, eat your dinner off me…' But while I was thinking about running my hands over his six-pack, he was still detailing his exercise routine. 'And at the weekends I swim at least sixty lengths of the municipal pool. But it's all worth it, wouldn't you say?'

'Er – yes,' I said, reaching for a tortilla chip and loading it up with salsa. The look he gave me as I popped it into my mouth bordered on horror.

'You don't want to touch those things,' he said. 'Nutritionally, they're complete rubbish. Now, me, I stick to a high-protein, low-carb diet. Lots of fruit and veg, and two litres of water a day. I don't even normally touch alcohol, but tonight I thought I'd have a small cup of this stuff as a treat and then I'll be on orange juice for the rest of the night.'

I kept up a façade of looking interested, but I was still trying to think of a way to bring the conversation round to a more carnal level. He might be a fitness bore, but I was willing to overlook that if I knew he was also into kinky sex.

'Well, as long as that means you've got a lot of stamina,' I said. 'Because that's what I like in a man. Someone who's big enough and strong enough to pin me down in any position. Tell me what to do, you know the kind of thing...'

The way he was looking at me I knew that, frankly, he didn't have a clue what I was talking about. Here was I, practically begging to be dominated and fucked till I could barely stand, and he was more interested in how many calories there were in the guacamole.

It was no good. I was talking to a bloke with the body of a Greek god, but the brain of a Greek salad. Desperately, I looked round for someone to rescue me before Darren bored me into a coma, and caught the eye of a man I hadn't noticed before. It was surprising, given that he must have been the tallest person in the place but then, in the admittedly well-cut suit and black shirt he was wearing, he didn't exactly stand out among all the cartoon characters and teenage wet dream superheroes. He smiled at me, and I wondered just how much of our conversation he had overhead.

Darren excused himself to get a glass of orange juice and the stranger wandered over. 'Haven't you learned yet that the first rule of playing mind games is you have to do it with someone who's got a mind?' he asked.

Damn, so he knew exactly what was going on – or, rather, not going on – between me and Darren. I made a point of eyeing his suit up and down, trying to ignore that with his tufty brown hair and clear hazel eyes, he was actually rather handsome. Not in Darren's league admittedly, but still not bad.

'Don't tell me,' I said, 'your hero is your bank manager.'

He smiled. 'No, I was actually going to come as Neil Armstrong, but then I got stuck in a meeting with clients

160

and I didn't have time to go home and change. So I just turned up as I was. I know it looks like I haven't made an effort, but if anyone asks, I'm searching for the hero inside myself.'

It was a good line and it made me laugh, even though I suspected he had been rehearsing it on the way over here.

'So how do you know Tony?' he asked.

'I don't,' I said. 'He's my friend's boss. You might have seen her – she's the one dressed as Wonder Woman.'

'Oh, yeah, she's in the kitchen, wrapped all round Luke Skywalker. When I went in there, it looked like she was having a play with his light sabre.' He reached for the ladle in the punch bowl. 'More punch, or are you trying to keep a clear head for your brave warrior?'

I glared at him. 'You're not going to let this go, are you?'

'What, that you were more interested in the size of the package than what was inside it?' He ladled punch into my cup and I took a sip, wondering how much of the stuff it would take to blot out my memory of the night's humiliation. The stranger's next words made me realise that might not be the best option. He bent the considerable distance which was required to get down close to my ear and murmured, 'Because you have to realise that some of us do know the kind of thing you were talking about…'

My words came back to me: 'Pin me down. Tell me what to do.' I shivered; I couldn't help myself.

'Why don't we go into the bedroom and talk about this further?' he suggested.

I drained my cup. 'OK, but why don't you tell me your name first?'

'It's Marc,' he said, 'but you can call me sir.' From the tone of his voice, he wasn't joking. That was fine by me. I didn't want jokes. I wanted someone who would play the game on my level, and it seemed that was exactly what

161

Marc had in mind.

I had thought the bedrooms might all be occupied, but Gillian's boss had a big house which Marc clearly knew his way around, and, anyway, it didn't appear to be that kind of party. We found a small guest room on the third floor. There was a key in the lock and Marc made sure to turn it, so we would not be disturbed.

I stood looking at him, stomach churning with lust and nervousness. I wanted Marc to take control, but part of me was still Lara, the defiant heroine, and felt the need to put up some kind of resistance. 'So tell me just why you've brought me up here,' I said, hands on hips.

'I'll tell you – but only once you've taken that T-shirt off,' he said.

So this was what he had in mind: take away what power I had in the situation by stripping me. The thought of baring myself for him was making my juices flow, but still I stood there, defying him.

'Do as I tell you.' His voice was low, authoritative. 'Or I'll take it off you myself and make you walk back into that party topless.'

The images he was planting in my mind almost made me whimper. His big hands, tearing the clothes from my back while I made a half-hearted attempt to stop him… I stared at him for a long moment, then pulled off the T-shirt and threw it on the bed. Under it, I was wearing a push-up bra, bulked out with a couple of handkerchiefs to give me something approaching a decent cleavage, though nothing as pneumatic as that of my computer-generated alter ego.

'That, too,' Marc demanded. Again I feigned reluctance for a moment then gave a little sigh and let the bra join the T-shirt. Marc didn't say anything as he gazed at me, but his expression told me how much he appreciated the sight.

He came to stand behind me, cupping my breasts in his hands. I was aware of how big he was, how confident –

how much more of a man than Darren, whose charms were entirely on the surface.

'So what does the rest of your little fantasy involve?' Marc asked, squeezing my nipples. 'You're in a room with a strange man, half-naked, helpless – what happens next?'

Where did I start? I had imagined a moment like this so many times. I had plenty of dirty games I wanted to play, plenty of roles I wanted to adopt, but I settled for the thought my first view of Darren had awoken in me. 'I want to be made to suck your cock – sir.'

He laughed. 'I think that's easy enough to arrange.' He pushed me away from him, ordered me on to my knees. I obeyed, waiting as he unzipped his fly and brought out his cock. He gripped it and began to rub. As I watched, it stiffened into life. When he was satisfied it was hard enough, he caught hold of my ponytail and brought my face up to the level of his groin. 'Suck me,' he demanded.

I took hold of him, fed the head of his cock into my mouth. The fact he was still fully dressed, still outwardly respectable, whereas I wore nothing but my boots and shorts, now tangibly damp at the crotch, made me feel delightfully vulnerable. I almost wished that he had dragged me back into the party and forced me to worship him orally in front of all the other guests. As my tongue continued to play up and down the length of him, I sneaked a hand down into the waistbands of my shorts so I could touch myself.

He spotted what I was doing immediately. 'Did I give you permission?' he asked.

'No, sir,' I replied automatically.

'Well, stop it, then. You don't come until I say so. Now keep licking, slut.'

That did it. The use of the word slut, so deliberately demeaning, seemed to wake something within me, something dark and thoroughly deviant. I did as he wanted, sucking him till my jaw ached and I was convinced he was

163

about to shoot his come down my throat. That was when he pulled away and hauled me on to the bed.

Before I could protest, he had turned me on to all fours and yanked my shorts and knickers down to my knees. 'Stay like that,' he ordered me. 'I want to get a good look at both your holes.'

The crude choice of words, intended to reinforce the idea that I was nothing more than a series of orifices for his pleasure, reached right down to the deeply submissive side of me. I did as I was told, spreading my legs as widely as I could. It was not easy, given that they were still hobbled by my partially removed clothing, but I waited in that position, trying to imagine the view I might be giving him as he undressed rapidly.

The next thing I knew, he had climbed on to the bed behind me. He pulled my clothes the rest of the way off, and then I felt his fingers diving into the folds of my sex. He spread the wetness he found there around the entrance to my anal hole, gently stroking until I began to relax and he could slip the tip of a finger inside there.

'How would you like me to fuck you here?' he asked. 'Want me to bugger that tight little hole of yours?'

I gasped, wondering if he was serious, and then he said, 'No, we'll save that pleasure for another night.' While the thought that this might not be a one-off was beginning to sink in, I felt Marc's cock pushing at the entrance to my pussy. I reached behind me and helped guide him in. I had thought he might be too large for me, but I took almost all of him before he began to thrust into me. As I'd hoped, he set the pace – even now, he was firmly in control – and when he finally gave me permission to start rubbing my clit, I did so gratefully, more than ready to come given all the physical and verbal stimulation I'd received.

It seemed like only moments before he was speeding up and his hips were jerking in the unmistakeable manner of a

164

man who is about to come. That was the point at which he ordered, 'Come for me, Lisa. Come for me, now!' and I felt my pleasure peaking again and again, caught up in the sensations of my orgasm and his.

Minutes passed before I finally regained anything approaching composure, and when I untangled my body from Marc's, it was with regret.

We kissed, and he hugged me to him. 'Come on,' he said, 'we'd better go downstairs before people start wondering where we've got to.'

'It's all right,' I said, 'I'll just tell them you were arranging my overdraft for me.'

'I have not come as a bank manager!' Marc protested. 'And if you keep insisting that I have, you're just going to have to be spanked.'

'You wouldn't dare,' I said, in the brattiest tone I could manage, already thinking of how that particular scene might play itself out, and eager to find out if it was as good in reality as it was in my imagination.

As we walked back into the party, which was already beginning to wind down, I saw Darren in the corner, chatting up a girl who had come dressed as Jessica Rabbit. He was running his hand through his hair in the gesture which I had initially found so sexy but now realised was just one of the tricks in a very limited repertoire. Suddenly, I was so very glad that I had done the right thing. I had held out for a hero, and found one where I least expected it. I raised my water pistol to my temple in an ironic salute to the plastic warrior, and let Marc lead the way home to bed.

I Spy
by Jean-Philippe Aubourg

'Oh yes baby! Swing those hips baby! Shake that booty!'
Ben peered through his window at the highlight of his day.
The lithe large-breasted blonde who worked in the next-
door office block arrived and left within minutes of the
same time every day. He had no idea what her name was or
what she did for the eight hours Monday to Friday that she
spent in the building, but he did know that her figure floated
his boat.

Slim, without being skinny, her hips tapered up into a
wide bottom. She favoured trousers, which Ben thought
showed off her arse perfectly. Her breasts seemed to be a
mirror image of her bum, large and round. They bounced
beautifully as she walked past Ben's booth in the car park.
One morning she had been late, and he'd found himself
wondering where she was. Then she appeared, running. She
had both hands clasped to her breasts to keep them under
control as she jogged from her Ford Fiesta. It was one of
Ben's briefest glimpses of her, but also one of his most
exciting.

Never the most eloquent of men, Ben had nicknamed the
object of his affections 'Blondie Big Tits'. He had precious
little intellectual stimulation in his job as the car park
attendant, and he looked forward to seeing her jaunty little

walk at the start and end of his boring days, plus two more sightings every lunchtime. If only he could find a way of taking the image home, to replay it over and over again?

The answer came during one of his long periods of boredom. His new mobile. It had a built-in camera which would even take videos. He had nothing else to photograph or film, and how difficult could it be?

He practised a few times, keeping it on standby, then picking it up as a nondescript pedestrian passed, quickly pointing and pressing the button. The results improved with each attempt, until finally he felt ready for the big challenge.

The first day he got it completely wrong. She was early, he wasn't ready, and by the time he had fumbled with the phone she had vanished. The second day she was late, and he was distracted by a query from another driver, which Ben dealt with in an even less enthusiastic manner than usual.

Finally he got it right. Blondie arrived at her usual time, wearing tight trousers and a short tailored jacket plus heels that gave her a little bit of extra bounce. As she passed, Ben picked up the phone. His hand followed her movements and he watched with pleasure, as her image appeared on the screen. His hand trembled a little as he watched it getting smaller and smaller, until she had vanished round the corner, and he pressed stop.

He spent the morning replaying the clip, enjoying Blondie's sexy walk over and over. He became so absorbed he almost forgot time was pushing on to twelve-thirty, when his target would be off for lunch. He put the phone on standby again and waited. Sure enough, her swaying figure came past, heading back to her car, before climbing in and driving to wherever she went for her break. Ben caught it all on camera, only a few seconds, but enough to double his enjoyment.

An hour later it was trebled when she returned, and Ben captured another lingering shot of her retreating bottom. He spent the afternoon watching the clips and dreaming of the summer months, when he knew Blondie would wear tight tops with low cleavages, imagining how her heavy breasts would look wobbling towards the camera again and again.

Five o'clock came round much more quickly than usual, and Ben was poised with his mobile again. But there was no sign of her. Disappointed, he put the phone down. Quarter-past, but Blondie still failed to join the exodus from the car park. Five-thirty, and still her car sat in an ever-emptying concrete space. Five-forty-five, and by then it was virtually the only vehicle left. Just before six, and it was.

Wondering what on earth had happened to her, Ben thought about calling security. He was on duty till seven, and he was supposed to take an interest in any cars left after hours, even though employees could use their passes to get in and out without him. He was about to reach for the phone when the familiar click of heels checked his hand and made it scrabble for the mobile.

There she was, an hour late and evidently peeved about it, as she seemed to be stamping her feet as she walked. Not Ben's concern really, he just wanted a fourth angle on that superb arse.

And he got just that, with her bottom at first filling the viewfinder, then getting smaller as she headed to her car. But then Blondie stopped, turned around and walked back, but not to the office. She was heading directly towards Ben's cubicle.

It so happened that Ben had chosen this opportunity to test the camera's zoom facility. He had been having some success too, and had managed to get the shaky image homed in on Blondie's bottom. So, when she turned around, it was suddenly focussed on her breasts, which quickly became blurred as she stalked towards him.

Ben quickly dropped the phone, to find Blondie's face framed in his window. Her pretty features scowled straight at him. 'What the fuck are you up to?' she demanded.

Ben opened his mouth to answer, but couldn't get any words out. Taking his silence as an admission of guilt, Blondie yanked open the door and strode in. Grabbing the phone from his paralyzed fingers, she pressed stop, then play. She watched the footage he'd just shot, then flicked through the gallery, finding the rest.

The furious woman held the phone up. 'Did you seriously think I wouldn't spot you, making your clumsy little videos? As a peeping tom you're absolutely hopeless.' For a second Ben thought about leaping through the window and running away across the car park – he was that embarrassed.

'I saw you the first time this morning. I hoped you'd be happy with one film, even though the thought creeped me out. But then you did it again at lunchtime, twice! I don't like being stalked by a pervert with a camera, so I waited till everyone was gone, to see if you'd do it again. Which you did!'

All the time Ben could feel his face throbbing with shame and humiliation. He ran through all the options he might be facing, and even to a man of his limited imagination, none of them seemed particularly good. They all involved unemployment, and at least one had him standing in court. But none of them were close to the actual sequence of events.

Pocketing the phone, presumably as evidence, Blondie closed the door and pulled the blinds. She looked directly at Ben. 'Trousers and pants off,' she said.

Ben did not believe what he had heard. Evidently that was what Blondie had expected, so she repeated the order, and added an explanation. 'I could report you, get you fired, maybe even get the police to explain the stalking laws to you, but I don't see why I should go to all hassle for a worm like you. On the other hand, you're not getting away with it – I'm taking the law into my own hands. Which is why I need your bum bare.'

Ben was bewildered, but knew he was out of choices. If he wasn't going to lose his job or be prosecuted, how bad could whatever Blondie was planning be? Trembling, he fumbled with his belt and trouser buttons, unzipped the fly and let them drop to the ground. 'Pants too' Blondie barked. He opened his mouth to protest, but she silenced him with an angry glare.

Burning with shame, Ben pushed his hands into the waistband and pushed his boxers to his knees. He stood, feeling the air blowing around his genitals, which were shrivelled with apprehension. The irony of how many times he had dreamt of undressing with Blondie in the room wasn't lost on him, but in his imagination his member had always been proud and erect. The situation wasn't helped by her staring straight at them. 'What?' she sneered, 'don't my tits and bum give you a hard-on? I thought that was what all the fuss was about!' Ben could feel tears welling up in his eyes. 'Right, bend over, hands on that desk, bum well out'.

As she spoke, she pulled the chair away to make room for Ben to do as he was told. When he was in position she slipped her jacket off. Looking at her over his left shoulder, Ben saw the swell of her chest, and could not help but admire it, despite his predicament.

Rolling the right sleeve of her blouse to her elbow, Blondie stood on Ben's left side, and placed her palm on his right cheek. By now he had worked out what she in mind, even if he could not quite believe it.

'So, you like spying on women, do you, you filthy little pervert? Well, I'm going to teach you a lesson you won't forget in a hurry!' She quickly pulled back her arm, and brought it down hard, slapping his bottom hard. Ben let out a cry of shock and pain, and moved to stand, but a firm push in his back from Blondie's left hand sent him back over the desk. 'We can go and discuss your behaviour with human resources, if you prefer? No? Thought not!' A second slap landed on Ben's other buttock. So ashamed was he at being caught red-handed, it never occurred to him to suggest discussing HER behaviour with human resources!

The spanking continued apace, Blondie clearly angry at the liberty Ben had taken. He groaned at each stinging slap, and at the growing heat in his bottom. But something strange was also happening down there. He had no idea why, but he could feel his penis becoming hard.

Whether Blondie had noticed or not, it had no effect on her stroke. Slap – slap – slap – slap! Her palm alternated from one buttock to the other, the spanks getting harder each time. But as they got harder, so did Ben.

Eventually she stopped. Standing back with her hands on her hips, she ordered Ben to stand up and turn around. He did so, and was faced with the sight of her heaving breasts, as she brought her breathing under control. That was all too much for him, and his erection rose to full power, twitching and pointing directly at the object of his lust.

'Good God! You have no shame! Well I'm not doing this for your weird pleasure! Get rid of it!' Ben looked at her, not understanding what she meant. She clarified herself. 'I mean, with your hand! Like I assume you always have to!'

It was almost a relief for him. His brain had passed control to his member and now, no matter how embarrassing his position, he had to give it attention.

He began to masturbate, groaning and sighing almost as much as he had done under punishment. Blondie obviously wanted him to get it over with quickly. 'Come on! Come for me! Imagine getting your hands on this for real!'

Turning her back to him, she wiggled her bottom, the root cause of this whole bizarre situation, now being flaunted just a few feet from Ben.

His hand flew up and down his length at astonishing speed. She ran both hands over the seat of her trousers, tightening the material against the ball of flesh, and he was gone. His seed blasted from his rod and splashed onto the vinyl tiled floor.

About a minute later he looked down at the sticky mess, then back up at Blondie. He was astonished to see she was facing him again, now with the thick leather belt that had been looped around his own trousers. 'Back over the desk!' she snapped.

Ben obeyed with a sob. 'I wasn't having you enjoying this' she told him. 'I'm giving you twelve, and they're going to bloody hurt!' Taking hold of the belt half-way up its length, she tapped the red bottom she now intended to make redder. Raising her arm, she brought it down with a whipping movement, cracking it across the raw meat.

'Aaagh!' he wailed. She showed him no mercy. The second blow landed almost straight away, burning its way to the core of his being. He was not keeping count, but Blondie obviously was. After the twelfth stroke had slapped across his agonised bottom, she threw the belt down with his discarded trousers and boxers.

Ben sank to his knees, desperately rubbing his cheeks with both hands. He was vaguely aware of Blondie pulling down her sleeve, putting her jacket on and picking up her handbag. She took Ben's phone out of her pocket, looked at it and pressed a few buttons. Then she tossed it onto the desk beside him.

'All evidence of your pervy lechery erased' she said. 'The evidence of how pissed off you made me could take a little longer to disappear'. They both looked at the livid weals, growing more vivid on Ben's cheeks by the second.

'And if I EVER catch you so much as looking at me again, I'll...well, just don't!'

As the door slammed behind her, Ben struggled to make himself respectable, and wondered why something so dangerous, painful and humiliating had been one of the most intense and exciting experiences of his life.

My Good Boy
by Sommer Marsden

The first time I saw Joshua he was stumbling down the Avenue at twelve in the afternoon. Snookered, drunk, high as a kite. He was wearing a three-piece suit that any fool could tell cost a pretty penny. I'm not one for suits but even I wanted to run my hand over that dark grey fabric. I just knew it would feel like liquid silk. His shaved head radiated a lobster-like glow from the alcohol and he was smoking a cigarette in *that* way. The way an extremely plastered person smokes. Not just smoking it, but drawing on the filter so hard I half expected him to suck the entire smouldering cylinder into his mouth.

I was drawn to him. I admit it. He positively radiated submissive. This was a man who felt out of control and he needed some help. Some tender loving care. Or a good whipping. It was a toss-up.

My feet carried me to him before I could reconsider. I was hoping I had struck gold. A man who carried the weight of the world on his shoulders but craved a woman who would push him. And push him around. I get off on power. I get off on men who can be broken. For whatever reason, I wanted to get off with this man.

'What's wrong with you?' I said down to him. He was sitting on a concrete planter that held a sickly-looking palm tree. 'Why are you fucked up at noon?'

I figured it best to let him see exactly who I was right off the bat. If he was going to be mine, then he had to see the real me from the get-go.

He squinted up at me and took another severe drag on his cigarette. 'I am not drunk,' he said very carefully. The caution and slow speech obviously earmarked him as a completely bombed individual.

'You most certainly are,' I sighed and planted one of my black stiletto heels on the planter. His eyes were level with my crotch and my short skirt rode up with the movement. No doubt he had a perfectly wonderful view of my crotch. That was good.

'OK, so I am,' he said directly to my pussy.

'Good. At least you're being honest. Now tell me why,' I barked. Oh, if only I had a whip. Hell, I'd settle for a ruler.

'I am...' he slurred, '...having a bad day. I have too much stress. I feel like I might...' he trailed off and took a final drag of his cigarette, practically licking the fucking thing. I snatched it out of his fingers and flicked it into the street.

'Explode? Cry? Jump off a large building?'

'Yesh,' he sighed. 'All of the above.'

'Come on,' I said and grabbed his hand. I hauled him to his feet and stood there waiting for him to fall over or fall on me. He did neither.

'Where're we going?'

'You're coming home with me and we are going to get you straightened out.' I marched him toward my waiting Jeep.

'You don't even know me!'

I stopped turned and said, 'Diane. And you are?'

'Joshua Davies.'

'Good. Now I know you. Get in the fucking car,' I said and pointed to the door. He nearly broke his neck getting in but he managed.

I could not wait to get him home.

He slept the twenty-minute drive to my house. He was snoring to the point of annoyance and I knew the first thing I'd make him do was brush his teeth. Stale beer breath is not a turn-on.

I pulled into the driveway and unbuckled. Went around and opened the passenger side door. 'Joshua!' I barked.

He came awake in a series of grunt and snorts. He blinked at me and wiped his mouth. 'We here?'

'Yes. Get out. Let's go.' I helped him out, though. The last thing I needed was for him to take a header in the driveway and knock himself unconscious.

Inside, I set about making a pot of coffee in case he'd need it. 'There are towels in the linen closet. The bathroom is the last room down the hall. Get a towel, take a shower and brush your teeth. Use my toothbrush, I'll get a new one.'

Now I waited. Was he what I thought he was? Most men would tell me to fuck off. Or complain or try to hump me in the kitchen. He dropped his head and nodded. 'OK.'

I smiled. I could smell them a mile away. 'Well? Why are you just standing there? Get moving.'

By the time he came out of the shower, his skin pink like a baby, I was in my corset and boots. My big red boots. They make me feel like a superhero. I love boots. In a sexy pair of boots I feel like I can beat the devil.

He gaped at me. His eyes skittering over the boots, the corset, the stocking, the thong. They settled on the thong, widened, shot back to the boots, widened further.

'Better be careful or they'll pop right out of your head,' I said softly and then brought the whip from behind my back

177

and gave it a crack. I made it snap and sing to show him what he was in for.

He grew pale but his cock bobbed to life in an instant. I managed not to laugh but I did smile. 'Ready?'

'Yes,' he said and swallowed hard.

'Yes, what?'

'Yes, ma'am.'

Ah. A boy who had been raised with manners.

'Rules,' I said and cracked the whip again. 'You give me a word that you will use if you want me to stop. My rule is, if I stop, then we are done. Not just for the day. For good. However, I will stop at any time if you give me the word. What's your word?'

He blinked and cleared his throat. 'Pressure,' he croaked.

'Good. Now let's go. Leave your towel on the floor and follow me.'

In the living room, I pointed to my grand-mamma's ottoman. Covered in faded brocade with a lovely sea green fringe, it was so very proper, and the perfect height for whipping a man's ass a lovely cherry red. I pointed but didn't speak and Joshua complied without direction. Had he done this before? I wondered. Either way, I would know in a moment.

He draped his broad chest and flat stomach over the top of the ottoman so that the edge was flush with his hip bones. Instinctively, he gripped two of the legs on the ottoman. He thrust his ass high for me, knees together, feet flexed, head down. Nice.

'Count them off. Be polite.' Let's see what he did with those directions.

I went slow with the first one even though the crotch of my panties was already wet. Just the anticipation of hearing the whip slice and whistle through the air was enough to make me hot. It was the most sensual sound I could think of. With the toe of my boot, I forced his ass a little higher and took the time to run the soft leather low enough to stimulate his sac. He moaned and it made me want to moan.

I reared back with my hand, gulped a deep breath and let it unroll through the air with a nice sibilant swish. The sound of the leather biting his skin beaded my nipples instantly.

His head flew back and he grunted. Like magic the stripes appeared on the pale flesh of his ass. 'One, ma'am.' He sounded almost calm, number two was harder.

'Two, ma'am!' he barked and a flood of fire burned under my skin. I felt the flush of power creep across my breast and chest bone. I felt it snake around my throat and heat the back of my neck.

I let the whip fly with its own ferocity. It knew what it was doing. The tendrils danced across his skin. The marks crosshatched white, red, pink. Little dots of purple in the mix. A shiver worked through me and my pulse beat between my legs. I rubbed my thighs together and felt the wet fluttering in my cunt.

'Three, ma'am!' Joshua threw his head back, teeth gritted, tears seeping from the corners of his eyes. Beautiful, big green eyes. He looked tortured and serene. Ethereal and demonic. All those at once and then some.

The breath tore in and out of him as the whip and I rained blows down upon him.

Four...six...eight...

I paused briefly, toeing his thighs apart some so I could see his balls. I pushed them hard with my foot and he arched back against my boot shamelessly. I nudged his perineum just enough to make him jitter a little. The sound that escaped him was that of a desperate animal.

'How hard is your cock, Joshua?' I demanded, stepping back and regaining my stance. We were about to finish up.

'Very hard.'

'Very hard, what?' I growled and gave him the hardest lash yet. His body did a dance that looked like a seizure.

'Very hard, ma'am! Nine,' he sobbed, his forehead pressed deep into the cushion.

'Don't forget your manners, boy.'

I delivered the final lash. So hard and fast my wrist ached from the force.

'Ten…' he said in a whoosh of air. His body bucked and he sobbed openly as I stared at the vibrant marks on his bone white ass.

Power and need sizzled through me. And I fingered myself as I watched him. Broken and weak but humping my grandmother's ottoman for all he was worth. Mindless at this point. Lost somewhere in that gray area that lives between extreme pain and extreme pleasure.

I pulled Grand-mamma's chair up to the ottoman. The old fabric threadbare in some spots. As far as design, the chair was perfect. I took off the thong but that was it. After all, this was our first time. I sat, threw a leg over each cushioned arm and bared myself, opened wide.

'Slide that up here, Joshua, and eat me. And this better be good.'

He scooted forward eagerly, pushing the ottoman across the hardwood floor. His face was pale and drawn but his eyes were burning fiercely in his face. He pushed into me without preamble. Tongue seeking my clit blindly, suckling, swirling. Slow licks, fast licks, broad tongued and pointed. His mouth was a blur of hot, wet movement over my clit and lips. I let my head fall back and in my mind I heard the sinister whisper of the whip during descent. The echo of remembered sound mixed with his exuberant, noisy, ministrations. I grabbed his smooth, shiny head and fucked his mouth until I came. The muscles of my legs jumping from the force and intensity of what that tongue could do.

'Who's my good boy?' I said softly. My eyes finding his and holding his gaze.

He looked away, blushing the same lobster-red shade he had been when I met him. 'I am, ma'am.'

'Joshua is,' I corrected.

'Joshua is your good boy,' he amended.

'He is. And my good boys get rewarded.'

I moved around behind him and covered his body with mine. His cock was hard and long in my hand. He had as much girth as length and my mouth watered at the thought of sucking him. My cunt thumped at the thought of riding him. My ass ached to feel that much filling me. But I don't do things that way. Not the first time. All of those would come. Most likely before I dropped him off at his car later. But the first time, they never get what they want.

I wet my hand with my own juices, and, with my palm slick from my orgasm, I started slow and easy. Stroking him, jacking him off. I squeezed and released. Alternated fast and slow. Kept him just on the edge as I ground my naked pelvis against his sore ass.

Joshua tensed under me and I said softly, 'Not yet. I haven't told you that you could yet.'

He stayed tense, his breathing harsh. He moaned off and on as if he were in pain. Maybe he was.

I rolled my thumb over the sensitive crown, gathered the drop of pre-come from his weeping slit. When I couldn't stand it any more, I started a fast steady pace and when his body signalled to me I shouted, 'Come now, Joshua.'

So well-behaved. He covered my hand with thick, hot ropes of his come. The bleach-like scent of semen filled the air. I raised my hand to his face and I didn't have to say a word. He licked it clean. His tongue warm velvet on my skin as he tongued my hand clean. I shivered when he sucked my fingers into his mouth and moaned.

Now that he was sober, we had the rest of the day ahead of us. 'My good boy,' I cooed, 'we're just getting started.'

Bathtime
by Chris Skilbeck

Melissa lies back into the warm foamy water, sighing with pleasure as she feels the silky wetness gliding over her body. She takes a sip of her wine and closes her eyes.

It's a rare treat; Mick is out for the whole day and she's already done all the housework she intends doing. The bathroom curtains are closed, softening the late morning sunshine to a lovely golden glow. Gentle music carries from the sitting room.

Melissa has scented the water with ylang-ylang; she adores the warm sensual aroma. She slides her hands slowly over her breasts, smiling at the prompt reaction of her nipples. She reaches over the edge of the bath for her towel and dries her hands before picking up her mobile. On her contact list it just says 'C'; she presses the call button.

'Hi, Mel. Good to hear you. How's things?'

'Good; things are very good. He's out. Come round; the door's unlocked and I'm in the bath. Remember what I told you?'

'Damn right I do – I'll be round in ten minutes.'

'Good boy. Remember everything I told you, now.'

'I will. See you soon.'

Melissa turns the phone off and drops it onto the bath mat. She picks up the sleep mask and puts it on, fitting it carefully. She tries to relax. With one hand she caresses her breasts gently, keeping her nipples firm and wanting more. Her other hand moves down, down over her tummy, sliding smoothly in the foam. She traces the edges of her labia, trying not to think of when he might arrive – what he's going to do.

Was that a sound in the hall? Melissa strains her ears, holding her breath to keep silent. The music and her own pulse is all she can hear. She is so tense that she might burst with excitement; her hands are still. No further sound comes; she cannot hold her breath any longer and has to make herself lie back again, to breathe normally.

There is a moment of uncertainty – what if someone else were to come in? The unlocked door was the only thing she didn't like about the arrangement. She'd thought of giving him a key but there was no way he'd be able to get in silently that way.

Surely more than ten minutes had gone since she called him? Any moment now he'd be with her. He could be there now, looking through the open bathroom door, watching the back of her head.

Melissa wonders for a moment if she shou–.

His hands are big and strong and he holds her wrists together easily with one while covering her mouth with the other. She has barely realised what is happening before he has wrapped something silky around her wrists, tying them tight. She opens her mouth to object, this wasn't part of the plan, only the blindfold, but before she can find words he's wrapping a gag around her face; it pulls between her lips and he ties it firmly.

She is bound, unable to see or speak. His big hands roam across her back, up and down her spine. She is suddenly in a panic – this isn't exactly what she expected – can she be sure it's him? Anyone could have . . .

No, don't be stupid, of course it's him. He says nothing

but she can hear him breathing heavily, excited. She sits tensely upright in the warm water. Those big hands caress and coax. Of course it's him; she relaxes. As her body loses its tension his hands move down, under her breasts. He lifts them comfortably, caressing and stroking. She anticipates the feel of his fingertips finding her nipples.

He releases one breast and lifts the other one more firmly, pulling the under-skin tight and pushing the nipple upward without touching it. His other hand touches her again, sliding down from her shoulder, down onto the upper slope of the lifted breast. Melissa is holding her breath as his fingertips reach the outer edge of her nipple. She can feel it is erect, hard as a nut, aching to be touched – no, not just touched – pulled, rolled hard between strong finger and thumb-mauled.

His fingers move all around her nipple, nudging the edges of the engorged flesh, pushing towards the centre but . . . she cries her frustration through the gag as he releases her breast.

He lifts her other breast in the same way, pushing up the nipple. It responds eagerly as his fingers slide down towards it. Now, oh now, please, touch it! But he teases even more mercilessly this time; he circles and nudges with finger and thumb, taking tiny pinches of the skin of her areola.

He dips his hands into the bath, and lifts handfuls of warm water, letting it run over her breasts. Then he leans close and blows across her wet nipples. The sudden chilling is delightful for a second and then a torture. Her nipples are so tight she can feel the pulling in the surrounding skin. She chokes back a sob of desire and feels the swelling of her labia, slippery now with their own moisture.

His hands are on her shoulders again and slide down her chest and this time – at last – he captures her nipples, tugging them firmly, gradually increasing the pressure.

185

After the long build-up her pleasure is intense; her body quivers and she realises that the rapid panting she can hear is her own.

Melissa's nipples are hot and tender before he stops. He finally releases them and with his hands under her armpits he lifts her up out of the water, turns her, and pushes her hard against the cold tiles. Her breasts, so sensitive from his touch, are chilled and flattened. The sensation is fierce, almost painful, and it sends a spasm of need rippling from her nipples to her groin. Her screech – a howl of pleasure and frustration – escapes the edges of the gag.

After an excruciating moment he turns her round to face him. He holds her back against the wall and his lips and tongue take their greedy turn at her breasts. She can hear his ragged breathing betraying his own extreme excitement.

She shudders with anticipation as his head moves downwards.

He does not delay; his hands cup her buttocks, pulling her forward, and he pushes his face between her legs, sucking in the whole swollen mound of her sex. His tongue squirms between her inner lips and slides up to find the hard bud of her clitoris.

She almost faints with the sensation. His hands squeeze and knead her flesh, holding her up and pulling her close to him as he ravages her with his mouth. His lips narrow their attention to her clitoris, and pull at it while his tongue flickers lightly over the very tip.

Melissa cannot hold it back; wave after wave of overwhelming pleasure ripples out from her clitoris, charging and clenching every muscle in her body. Finally she is spent and her weight slumps in his arms.

He lowers her back down into the water, and unfastens the gag. As her mouth falls open to take a deep breath he turns her head towards him.

The end of his cock is hot in her mouth, already slippery

186

and salty, close to coming. She has never done it like this before; she's always been in control. Now, with her hands still bound behind her she feels him take a handful of her hair and set the pace. He moves her head back and forth gently – slower than she'd have done it – and he gives her only the swollen head of his cock. She sucks, and moves her tongue on the turgid flesh, feeling the energy of it, the tight, about-to-burst vitality.

He holds back, gasping, pulling her mouth away. Melissa strains forward against his grip, wanting him back in her. He submits, releases her hair. The only contact between them now is this concentration of tense pleasure, yet she senses his every nerve focussed there between her lips, on her tongue.

She holds him, his whole being, body, mind and soul, right there between the edges of her teeth. The lightest pressure is all it takes to hold him absolutely still. She flickers the tip of her tongue, barely touching him, teasing, threatening, promising.

After only a few seconds he can bear it no longer, Melissa hears him gasp – almost sob, 'Please!'

She moves slowly, as he'd done, sucking gently, then harder, then gently again. She hears him moan and then feels it too, vibrating through his cock, a deep animal note of pleasure.

His cock hardens and swells to that final urgent engorgement and Melissa's tongue feels the pulsing flow of his semen. The musky male taste fills her mouth. She continues to suck gently, giving him the longest pleasure she can as he grunts his satisfaction. He lays a gentle hand gratefully against her cheek – moves her slower, slower, slower – back and forth on his still-pulsing cock until at last he sighs and releases her.

He bends down and kisses her. His teeth nip gently at her lips; his tongue slips into her mouth, gently probing. His

187

hands slide easily down her body again, smoothing and settling her. She feels his fingers tugging at the bonds round her wrists; once they are free she feels nothing more of him. A minute or two later she hears the faint snap of the latch as he leaves, locking the door behind him.

Melissa sits quietly in the bath, listening to the music. Eventually she reaches up and pulls off her blindfold. Barely opening her eyes she reaches for her wine and takes a sip.

Melissa lies back into the warm foamy water, sighing with pleasure.

The Motor Mechanic
by Stephen Albrow

Juliet liked to look her best in every situation – even when she was only picking up her car from the mechanic's. She threw open her wardrobe, then put on her favourite red blouse, before reaching for her black satin miniskirt. She had already put on some black hold up stockings, but she wasn't quite sure if the mini would be long enough to cover the lacy tops. A quick check in the mirror said the skirt was long enough... but only just! It was just the effect she was looking for, so she slipped on her stilettos and then went downstairs.

Juliet's handbag was lying on the sofa, so she picked it up and checked what was in her purse. The mechanic, Peter, had told her it would cost roughly £80 to fix the dent in the bodywork. She smiled as she remembered how handsome he had looked in his greasy, navy-blue overalls. He was tall and dark, with a well-defined torso. He was the type of man who could completely overpower a girl, so she decided to leave her purse at home.

As she walked to the garage, she wondered how Peter would react when she told him she couldn't afford to pay him. It would be obvious to him she was lying, because he had guessed straightaway that Juliet was very wealthy. The expensive pink convertible gave the game away, as did her stylish, designer clothing.

Juliet was a daddy's girl, who got whatever she wanted. She'd sensed that the mechanic had resented that about her, but she'd also sensed he fancied her. She'd noticed him checking out her breasts on more than one occasion. Daddy had paid for those, as well!

It was almost six o'clock, which was when the mechanic closed for the night, so Juliet hurried on down the street. She could see the garage just up ahead. The doors were wide open and her car was being lowered down from the ramp. Peter was working the machinery, and even from a distance she could see the oil and sweat-stains on his overalls. He'd obviously worked very hard that day, but hopefully he'd still have some energy left in his tank!

'I've come to collect my car,' said Juliet, stepping into the mechanic's workshop.

'It's just finished,' said Peter, who did a double-take when he saw Juliet's outfit. The breeze was ruffling the hem of her skirt, making it flounce around her stocking tops. And her blouse was tight, with maybe one too many buttons left undone, so as not to spoil the view of Juliet's newly bought-and-paid-for cleavage.

'The dent came out fine,' the mechanic said, trying to keep his mind on his job. He ran his hand across the surface of the bright pink convertible. He showed a tender touch, which made Juliet all the more eager to feel his hands upon her skin.

'It's like I never even crashed the thing,' Juliet giggled, then she watched as Peter went over to the desk in the corner and filled out a bill. There was a Pirelli calendar pinned to the wall in front of him, showing a semi-naked woman draped over a sports car. Juliet wandered over, attracted by the sensuality of the image, which made something stir inside her body. The hunky mechanic and

190

her provocative outfit had already caused her cunt lips to moisten, but this image took her arousal further, as she imagined herself in the model's place, draped across the sports car's bonnet.

'So that'll be eighty-five quid, including VAT,' said Peter, but the mention of VAT didn't kill the moment. Quite the opposite – Juliet had been eagerly waiting for the money talk to start, since it gave her a chance to be a bad girl.

'I didn't bring my purse,' she told the mechanic.

'That's fine,' said Peter, 'you can always pay me on–'

'Wait,' said Juliet, butting in. 'I didn't bring my purse on purpose, because I have no money. I can't afford to pay you. I let you do the work even though I couldn't pay.'

Peter's eyebrows rose out of curiosity, then he glanced at Juliet and then at her car. It was obvious she was loaded. It was obvious she was a daddy's girl. So why was she fighting over eighty-five quid?

'Look, maybe I can do it slightly cheaper,' mumbled Peter, uncertain what else to do in the circumstances.

'But don't you think I'm a bad girl?' asked Juliet.

'N-no!' stammered Peter, polite at first. But then he reconsidered: 'Well, maybe you are.'

'Yes, I am,' insisted Juliet. 'I'm a bad girl and I deserve to be punished.'

Bemused but interested, Peter looked up into Juliet's face, trying to make some sense of the strange situation. The girl appeared to be totally serious. A fantasy was taking place inside her head – one she seemed determined to play out to the full.

Unsure of his role in the fantasy, but attracted to the girl, Peter walked to the front of the garage. He shut the doors, which blocked out most of the sunlight, giving the place the air of a dimly lit dungeon. His back still to the girl, he heard the sound of Juliet's stilettos. They made a click-clack noise on the concrete floor, as she strode towards her pink convertible. She wasn't the first girl to try and seduce the hunky mechanic, but Juliet was different. She seemed to want something more than the usual hard, fast sex with a bit of rough.

'I need to be punished,' said Juliet, as Peter stepped towards her.

'Yes, you're a very bad girl for not paying,' he said, suddenly getting the measure of the girl's desires. At six foot plus, he was towering over her, so it wasn't difficult for him to adopt a dominant manner. He gazed down at her, a scowl on his face, his rugged good looks turning angry and mean.

'Tie me up and whip me,' said Juliet, licking her lips in anticipation.

'Tie you up with what?' asked Peter, so Juliet lifted her skirt and showed him her nylon stockings.

'And whip you with what?'

'Are you wearing a belt?'

'Yes, I'm wearing a belt.'

'So, whip me with that!'

Juliet kicked off her stiletto heels, then rolled her hold up stockings down. She handed them to Peter, who made her turn around and lean across the convertible's bonnet, like the sexy model in the calendar. As she stretched out her arms, Peter used the stockings to bind her wrists to the wing mirrors. He pulled the stockings tight, so they chafed her skin. She was thoroughly bound, which was just how she liked it!

Peter walked in front of the car, admiring Juliet's trussed-up body. She was positioned face down against the bonnet, with her bottom poking up into the air. Her tiny skirt had risen almost to the top of her thighs, but not high enough for Peter's liking. He lifted it a little further, only to find Juliet had no knickers on.

'What a slut!' said Peter, and the comment was enough to send a shiver of lust through Juliet's body. She stared into the windscreen. She could see her own reflection, plus that of the dark-featured mechanic, who was standing tall behind her, menacingly so. She watched him unbutton his dirty overalls, which immediately fell down to his waist. He wore a T-shirt underneath, which was caked with sweat, the dampness of the fabric making it cling tight to his pectorals.

Peter pulled the belt from his jeans, then formed a loop with the leather strap. Doubling the thickness of the belt would make it easier for him to handle, as well as doubling the intensity of every lash. He tested the makeshift whip against the palm of his hand, and just the sound of the slap was enough to set Juliet's nerves a-jangle. The muscles in her buttocks tensed up tight, as she readied herself for the first hard lash.

'You're a bad girl,' yelled Peter, as he raised his hand and then drove the leather strap into Juliet's bare behind. His biceps were huge, so there was power aplenty in the strike, which sent quivers of pain through Juliet's flesh. She screamed at the point of impact, her howls getting louder, as the mechanic followed straight up with another fierce strike. The thick leather strap smacked Juliet's arse cheeks, a red mark colouring her flesh where it struck.

'You're a bad girl and a slut,' Peter shouted, as he wielded his weapon of punishment again. The leather belt zipped and thrashed through the air, before striking Juliet's curvy arse. An agonising burst of pain shot up her back and down her thighs, spreading way beyond the point where the belt had made contact. Her entire body was feeling it now, including her pussy, which started to throb.

'Harder,' shrieked Juliet, as the growing sting in her arse cheeks added fuel to the mounting fire in her cunt.

'Yes, harder,' agreed Peter, his biceps flexing, as he delivered six quick strikes of the belt. Each new blow was harder than the last, leaving Juliet's rear-end red and sore. So, keen to find fresh flesh to whip, Peter trained the next lash on her upper thighs.

As leather met skin, the young girl shrieked, but was it a cry of pain or a cry of pleasure? Peter sniffed the air and smelled Juliet's cunt. It seemed the harder he whipped her, the hornier she became. He gave her thighs another firm lash, then watched her writhe around on the bright pink bonnet. He saw a spasm of tension shoot through Juliet's body. He saw her wrists pull at the stockings that held her in place.

'You dirty fucking bitch,' the mechanic shouted, and how he longed to whip her again. He wanted to hear her squeal once more, and to leave another red mark on her buttocks and thighs, but his dick was too pumped up with tension. Peter *had* to fuck her now!

Excited, Juliet stared into the windscreen, watching as Peter threw aside the belt and dropped his overalls. He undid his jeans and stepped up behind her, pressing his erection between her cunt lips. His helmet was huge, but he forced it into her orifice, then thrust his full-length deep inside. The vigorous penetration made her gasp. Clearly he was still in dominant mode – out to teach her a lesson with his rigid dick!

'Filthy slut,' muttered Peter, as he started to power his manhood in and out of Juliet's cunt. His hands were gripped around her thighs, his fingers digging deeper, as his passion mounted with each new thrust. It was almost as if he was still whipping her. He wasn't tender and gentle or out to please her. There was aggression and venom in the way he fucked. Whipping Juliet had brought out the animal in him!

Juliet yelled, as Peter's cock went thumping through her pussy muscles. Her insides convulsed around his length, as he overwhelmed her with his visceral passion. She gazed at his reflection, in awe of his strength, of his handsome face and almighty prick. His dick was longer than any she'd known, but it was the girth that truly excited her. Never before had her cunt been made to stretch so far. Never before had her cunt been fucked with such unrelenting speed and force.

As Juliet's convulsions reached a near-orgasmic pitch, Peter put his all into one last thrust. He withdrew his helmet to the entrance of her cunt, then hammered his full-length straight back home, splitting her right down the middle with the blistering force of his carnal lust. Her climax was instant! Juliet threw back her head and roared with delight, as the spasms in her pussy went out of control. She could feel Peter's cockhead bulging inside her – the passionate thrust had made him climax, too. His dick was spitting out thick jets of spunk, which spurted into her orifice as forcefully as the leather belt had torn into her exposed cheeks.

'Let that be a lesson to you,' Peter said, still pumping his phallus back and forth. He could feel the orgasmic tension in Juliet's pussy, so was grateful for the moisture dripping from her gash. The extra lubrication allowed him to keep on thrusting through her tensed up muscles. He watched her reflection in the windscreen, as he drained his balls inside her cunt. He could see the look of fevered satisfaction in her eyes.

Peter tried again: 'I said, 'Let that be a lesson to you.'' But once again Juliet failed to respond. Deep sighs of pleasure were falling from her lips, as her cunt muscles pulsed around Peter's prick. Her orgasmic high was refusing to fade, since Peter had done such a perfect job of punishing her with his leather belt and, later, with his rock-hard prick. He had totally overwhelmed her with his masculine power, beating her into complete submission – just as she had hoped he would!

195

With her fantasy fulfilled, Juliet felt an urge to turn and kiss her master, but her wrists were still fastened securely in place. He was still the boss. He was still in control. And Juliet liked being Peter's bitch!

So, had she learned her lesson? Would she come back the next day with the money she owed him? Or would she leave her purse at home again?

Juliet already knew the answers to those questions, which is why her pussy was throbbing so hard. She hadn't learned her lesson. She was *such* a bad girl. Perhaps the naughtiest of them all! It was going to take a lot more whippings to get the badness out of her system! But she'd found the man to deliver the lashes. Peter would sort her out!

Imagine great sex on your doormat every month!

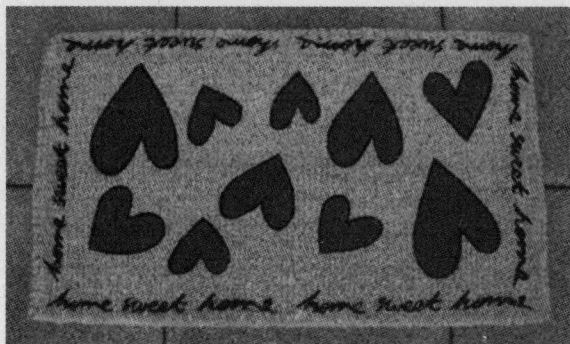

- Imagine a new Xcite book landing on your door mat every month.
- Imagine reading the twenty varied and exciting stories that each book contains.
- Imagine that three books are absolutely FREE as is the postage and packing.

**No hassles
No shopping
Just pure fun**

Yes! that's the Xcite subscription deal –
for just £69.99 (a saving of over £25) you will get 12 books
with free P&P delivered by Royal Mail (UK addresses only)

All books are discreetly and perfectly packaged
Credit cards are billed to Accent Press ltd

Order now at www.xcitebooks.com
or call 01443 710930

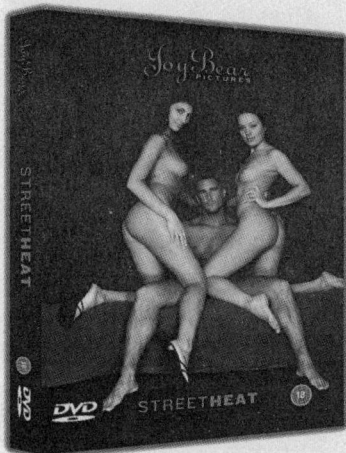
199

Also available from Xcite Books:
(www.xcitebooks.com)

Sex & Seduction	**1905170785**	**price £7.99**
Sex & Satisfaction	**1905170777**	**price £7.99**
Sex & Submission	**1905170793**	**price £7.99**
5 Minute Fantasies 1	**1905170610**	**price £7.99**
5 Minute Fantasies 2	**190517070X**	**price £7.99**
5 Minute Fantasies 3	**1905170718**	**price £7.99**
Whip Me	**1905170920**	**price £7.99**
Spank Me	**1905170939**	**price £7.99**
Tie Me Up	**1905170947**	**price £7.99**
Ultimate Sins	**1905170599**	**price £7.99**
Ultimate Sex	**1905170955**	**price £7.99**
Ultimate Submission	**1905170963**	**price £7.99**